Chapter 1

There is a place, a place where all of our sweetest thoughts and our kindest gestures go. Some people describe this world as a ray of sunshine wrapped in cotton candy, with a butterfly on top. . . . Others say this magical land is "made up" or "not real."

Well, we beg to differ. . . .

High above a lush green valley, two elegant storks flew gracefully across the bright blue sky. Their snow-white wings fluttered, causing the slightest breeze, as they soared toward a clearing just past a medieval village.

Riding the storks were Farmer Smurf and his friend, Greedy Smurf. They were on their way home after a successful morning picking Smurfberries.

"Whoooo-hooooo!" Farmer cried happily, as his stork made a sharp dive. "Oh yeaaaaaah!" He held tightly to an overflowing bag, careful not to spill any of the precious fruit.

"Come on, Farmer!" Greedy called out. Greedy's stork swept low and wove through a grove of ancient trees.

"Yeee-hah!!!" Farmer hollered, closely following Greedy's trail.

"I'm going in!" Greedy announced.

The storks dipped down, taking the two Smurfs on a thrill ride through the trees, over rocks, and across rocky ravines.

"Whoo-hooo!" Farmer shrieked with joy. He felt like he was riding a twisting and turning roller coaster.

Greedy was so high in the sky, he shouted out happily, "My ears just popped!"

Farmer brought his stork up alongside Greedy's. "All right, Greedy, I'm gonna race you!"

Greedy tightened his grip on the Smurfberry sack. "Whooa!"

The race was on! "Yes! Keep up with me, Farmer!" Greedy and his stork zoomed ahead.

"Whoo-whee!" Farmer replied with a chuckle. He flew his stork into a fancy barrel dive before zipping off after his friend. "Farm boys love to fly!" Farmer cheered.

"Oh yeah! I'm so excited!" Greedy said, seeing that Farmer was quickly catching up. "This is smurfin' great!" Greedy prodded his stork to go a little faster.

They quickly approached the clearing. "Now you see us . . . ," Greedy began, his stork diving low. It looked like it was about to land right there in the clearing, but it didn't land at all. Instead, Greedy and his stork vanished from sight. "Ha-ha! Now you don't!" Greedy's voice called out from beyond a shimmering mist.

Farmer chuckled. Leaning tightly into his stork's neck,

2

Farmer and Greedy flew down toward the clearing and straight through the glittery fog. "Three, two, one . . . oh!"

Farmer burst through the invisibility shield, into Smurf Village.

"Look how small the Smurfs look from up here! Oh, wait, we are small!" Greedy said. They flew above Smurf Village, side by side.

Smurf Village was smurfly glorious. Lush tall grass and wild blooming plants grew all around the small mushroom houses and shops. There was a bubbling river. Merry blue workers. And sunshine all day long. It was absolutely smurfect!

Greedy, Farmer, and the two storks soared above the town until they reached several large baskets.

"Oh yeah. I love Smurfberries!" Greedy said, diving low and releasing his berries into a basket below. "The blue ones are mine!"

Farmer giggled as he dumped his own bag of Smurfberries into the storage containers.

Greedy was so silly. All Smurfberries were blue. And the Smurfberries belonged to all the Smurfs.

In fact, they couldn't live without them. . . .

Chapter 2

Clumsy Smurf hurried across a bridge toward the center of town. "Oh smurf!" Clumsy exclaimed. "I'm late for rehearsal!"

In the distance he could see Smurfette, the only girl Smurf in the village, dancing under a banner that read: BLUE MOON FESTIVAL. Clumsy watched her leap like a ballerina through the air. Smurfette was then caught by a group of Smurfs on the stage.

"I'm sooo late!" he moaned, knowing that he should have been on that stage, helping to catch Smurfette.

The sound of flapping wings distracted Clumsy. Slowing his pace, he looked up. He paused for an instant as the two soaring storks carrying Farmer and Greedy sped through the sky.

A deep and booming voice caught Clumsy's attention: "Each and every Smurf has his or her own personality. Infused with love and sweetness."

Clumsy Smurf realized that Narrator Smurf had to be nearby. Then again, Narrator Smurf's loud voice traveled through the village easily. Narrator liked to explain what was going on and talk about things the Smurfs couldn't see for themselves.

But Clumsy was still focused on watching those Smurfberries fall from the sky. So focused, in fact, that he ran smack into Handy Smurf—*BAM!*

Handy was trying to fix the bridge. He'd been standing on a tall ladder when Clumsy hurried past. The ladder tipped when Clumsy blundered into it. Handy swung round and quickly grabbed for the side of the bridge, clinging on to the wooden rails for dear life.

"Sorry! Sorry, Handy!" Clumsy apologized. It was an accident, after all.

"No problem, Clumsy! You keep me employed!" Handy said.

Feeling confident that Handy was going to be all right, Clumsy continued on. He'd barely made it off the bridge when he managed to step onto an empty barrel that had been rolling in his path.

"Aaaagh!" Clumsy shrieked, struggling not to fall off as the barrel rolled him through the town.

Clumsy passed Painter Smurf working on a festival banner and sped toward Baker Smurf. "Hi, Baker! Nice pies!" Clumsy called out before accidentally bashing into Baker.

"Oof." Baker was knocked to the ground, but he was used to cleaning up after a Clumsy disaster. "Three-second rule, Clumsy!" he shouted after the barrel with a smile. Baker began to pick up and dust off his pies.

When the barrel hit a rock, Clumsy crashed. Luckily he wasn't hurt, but as he took his first step forward, Clumsy put his foot right into a pie that Baker had not yet scooped up. The pie filling was so slippery that Clumsy lost his balance. He tripped backward into Painter's festival banner, then bounced forward, flopping into an open wheelbarrow!

This was all normal for Clumsy, so he didn't fret.

"Lovely visit!" Clumsy called out to Painter just before the wheelbarrow rocketed down the road. "Can't stay! It's rehearsal time!"

"Whether it's Clumsy Smurf . . . Baker Smurf . . . Handy Smurf . . ."

This time Narrator really *was* nearby. He stood by the side of the road, speaking into a TV camera.

"Hey, Narrator Smurf!" Clumsy waved as he zoomed past in the wheelbarrow.

"Hey, Clumsy!" Narrator replied in his low, resonant TV voice. "Just rehearsing the intro for the Blue Moon Festival!" Narrator tugged at his turtleneck collar, cleared his throat, and continued to practice.

"Mmmm. Pizza!" Chef Smurf remarked as he crossed the street, carrying two pizzas. He was always admiring his gooey cheese-coated creations, and didn't notice Clumsy wheeling down the street.

Without warning, Clumsy's cart rammed into Chef. Chef fell into the cart, joining Clumsy on the ride. His gourmet pizzas flew up, high into the air.

"Clumsy!" Chef watched as his pizzas rocketed into the atmosphere.

The wheelbarrow hurried past Papa Smurf, the village elder, who watched it zip by like a speeding race car.

"Help!" Chef cried out, but Papa couldn't get there fast enough. Chef fell out of the wheelbarrow and landed with a crash. At that exact moment, his pizzas were landing too. With lightning reflexes, Chef scrambled to catch both pies.

Clumsy was still traveling in the wheelbarrow. "Sorry! I'll pay for that!" Clumsy called out, thinking that the pizzas were ruined.

Chef examined the pizzas, chilled from their trip into outer space. A smile crossed his face. There was no need for Clumsy to pay. "I just invented frozen pizzas!" Chef cheered. "Genius!"

Clumsy could only smile and nod since the wheelbarrow was now aimed at a table surrounded by some other Smurfs.

Clumsy shouted a warning. "Smurf on the loose!"

An instant later he hit the table at full speed and popped out of the wheelbarrow. When Clumsy landed on the tabletop, the Smurfs there were friendly and greeted him as he went surfing by. "Hey, Clumsy."

"Aaaaaaaagh!" Clumsy shrieked. He was out of control, headed straight toward Jokey Smurf's house.

Seconds later Clumsy tumbled in through Jokey's window and skidded across his kitchen table. "Hi, Jokey!"

Clumsy waved as he passed through.

"Hi, Clumsy!" Jokey greeted his fast-moving friend. The jokester had been busily putting prank toys inside yellow packages and tying them with red ribbons.

Clumsy somersaulted out Jokey's front door. And finally, like an Olympic gymnast at the end of a routine, Clumsy finished his wild ride through Smurf Village, landing firmly on two blue feet. Safe and sound at last!

"Who's clumsy now, huh?!" Clumsy announced, standing proudly outside Jokey's house. He dusted himself off, glad to be back on solid ground.

Jokey Smurf came outside.

"What do you get when you cross a Smurf with a cow?" Jokey asked. "Blue cheese!" Jokey Smurf began to laugh. "Ha-ha-ha-ha!" He held out a yellow package tied with a red ribbon. "I got you a present!"

Clumsy refused to take the box. "Oh—no thanks, Jokey! I'm late for rehearsal." Shaking his head, Clumsy began to rush away.

Jokey chased after him. "No, wait!" Suddenly the package erupted in Jokey's hands. Jokey looked at the torn and slightly burned yellow wrapping paper and the shreds of red ribbon. "Ha-ha-ha!" he laughed to himself.

Clumsy was very, very late to the Blue Moon Festival rehearsal. But by the time he reached the stage entrance, he was just relieved that he'd made it in one piece! Clumsy headed toward the practice, only to be stopped by Grouchy Smurf and Gutsy Smurf.

"Hey, Grouchy. Hey, Gutsy."

They were blocking his way. Behind the two Smurfs, Clumsy could see dozens of Smurfs practicing a song-and-dance routine. Clumsy tried to move past.

"Whoa, whoa, whoa! Slow your roll, sailor." Grouchy wouldn't let him go by.

Clumsy rose up on his toes to see behind Grouchy. "Wait, wait, wait. Isn't that the rehearsal for the Blue Moon Festival?"

On the festival stage Clumsy could see the Smurfs working out the steps to a musical number.

"Wonderful! Beautiful!" Vanity Smurf exclaimed, directing the dancers.

Only Vanity wasn't *actually* talking about the dance. He was talking about his own reflection in his handheld mirror. "Oh marvelous!" Vanity continued to praise himself.

In the hallway Grouchy looked down at the piece of paper he was holding, then shook his head. "What can I say, Clumsy, you're not on the list."

Squinting, Clumsy pointed to the paper in Grouchy's hands. "Grouchy, it's right there!"

Gutsy grabbed the list from Grouchy and took a look for himself. Then he showed Clumsy that his name was written there all right, just under a special heading. "It's under 'Do not let in.'"

Clumsy began to argue with both of them. That's when Brainy Smurf arrived. "Clearly you two lack the verbal skills required to explain this predicament succinctly," Brainy said.

Grouchy shook his head at Brainy and sighed. "Here we go."

"You see, Clumsy," Brainy began, ignoring Grouchy's comment. "The other Smurfs don't want to dance with you, for fear of what are politely called 'fractures.'"

"Awww, how could anybody think that?" Clumsy gestured wildly with his hands in the air, accidentally hitting both Grouchy and Gutsy in the face. "Ow!" Gutsy and Grouchy exclaimed at the same time.

Brainy shook his head. "That's going to leave a big, blue bruise!" he remarked, snootily. Then Brainy quickly took a step away from Clumsy and began to chuckle. There was no way he was going to get bruised too! But Gutsy and Grouchy each gave him a kick on his way out, just to be fair.

Brainy soared, up and up, like a football headed toward a goalpost. "Ahhhhh!" he screamed as he flew through the air. Finally he crash-landed on the stage, slamming into the dancing Smurfs, knocking them down like bowling pins.

"Hey!" one Smurf called from the bottom of the pile.

"Hey! What are you doing?!" another Smurf asked Brainy.

Vanity set aside his mirror. But only for a second. "Cut! Cut! Cut!" he said. "It's a dance, not dominos!" Vanity quickly picked the mirror back up and glared into it. "Ah! A worry line!"

Hefty Smurf flexed his big strong biceps. "All right,

don't get your petals in a twist." He began to dig Smurfs out of the heap.

With so many injured Smurfs, Clumsy wanted to help. He left the rehearsal and headed toward Papa Smurf's mushroom to get first aid supplies.

Meanwhile, just as the Smurfs got ready to try the dance again, Narrator Smurf showed up and reported some news:

"As happy and as perfect as life in Smurf Village is, even sunshine and butterflies must have their dark clouds. And for all Smurfs, that dark cloud has one name: Gargamel, the evil wizard."

Whack! Lightning cracked.

All the Smurfs on the festival stage looked up at the sky.

"Um . . ." Smurfette shivered in her high-heeled shoes. Her voice trembled. "All right, guys, let's get back to the rehearsal."

"Yeah, yeah, come on, guys. Let's do this," Hefty agreed, encouraging them to focus on the dance rehearsal.

Smurfette pulled herself together. She turned on the music and got back to business. "And smurf, six, seven, eight."

But Narrator was watching the ominous encroaching clouds and wondering what he'd be reporting next.

Chapter 3

Beyond Smurf Village, in the medieval town, a man sang the usually sweet Smurfs' song eerily off-key.

"La, la, la-la-la-la, sing a happy song . . ."

The scratchy, uneven voice wafted out through the chimney of a crumbling castle. The song was supposed to be a joyful, cheery tune. But for the evil wizard who sang it, the song wasn't joyful. It wasn't cheery either. It was depressing.

Because it reminded Gargamel of all the times he'd failed.

This time, Gargamel told himself, would be different. This time he'd capture the Smurfs. Very, very soon they would all be his prisoners!

Because this time, Gargamel had an excellent new plan.

"La, la, la-la-la-la, this is so wrong."

Gargamel stopped singing as he dangled two marionettes over an elaborate stage. The marionettes were carved out of wood. Their skin was painted bright blue, and big white eyes stood out on their faces. They were life-size, but they were still much smaller than Gargamel. They didn't even come up to his knee.

One of the puppets was an old man with a white beard and red clothes. The other was a young woman, in a white dress with matching heels. Moving the strings attached to the marionettes' hands and feet, Gargamel made the puppets dance around a large mushroom.

"Ooooh," Gargamel exclaimed in an overly cheery voice. "I'm Papa Smurf. I'm the head of a small group of blue people and live in the forest with ninety-eight sons and one daughter. Nothing weird about that. No, no. Totally normal."

Then in a high-pitched, flowery girl's voice, Gargamel made the other puppet say, "Ooooh, and I'm Smurfette. I think I'm sooo pretty. And I betrayed Gargamel and I don't even care. And everything is just sunshine and rainbows. Ha-ha-ha!"

Gargamel popped his head up and stood over the stage. He lowered his gnarled face and big nose closer to his two Smurf puppets. He was wearing an old black robe, worn through in some places and patched in others, and red, sturdy shoes that were specially made for chasing Smurfs. His crooked teeth showed through an evil grin, and the little hair he had, stood up on end.

In his own deep voice, Gargamel announced, "That's about to change!"

"Ahhhhh!" Gargamel cried, making the puppets scream and forcing them to cower at his greatness.

"I said, 'That's about to change,'" Gargamel repeated the line, looking over at his scraggily cat. "Azrael, that's your cue."

The orange cat stopped grooming himself and looked up lazily.

"That's your cue to pounce on the miserable beasts in some kind of a rage-induced feline frenzy!" Gargamel directed.

He dangled the puppets in front of the cat. Azrael swiped a sharp claw at the pretend Smurfs.

"That's good, yeah, more rage. But hey, don't go crazy, these are the only puppets I have."

"Meow," the cat replied, looking up at the sorcerer whose eyes twinkled with delight. Azrael knew what that look meant.

And Gargamel knew what Azrael's "meow" meant too. "I'm *not* obsessed with Smurfs, thank you. I simply can't stop thinking about the miserable beasts every single minute of every single day," Gargamel admitted, scanning the cavern filled with Smurf-related things.

Azrael asked, "Meow?"

"Because I need them!" Gargamel replied. "It is only by capturing the little wretches and extracting their happy blue essence that my magic will finally become . . . um . . ." Gargamel paused, unable to think of the right word. "Not *infallible* . . ."

The cat offered up a loud "Meow," correcting Gargamel's word choice.

Gargamel smiled a wicked grin. "Invincible! Yes, thank you."

"Meow."

"I shall become the most powerful wizard in all of the

world!" Gargamel broke into a fit of egomaniacal laughter. Azrael joined his master, laughing uncontrollably as well.

Gargamel stopped and stared at Azrael. "You're milking it. Don't milk it."

Returning to his play, the puppet master jiggled Smurfette's strings. "Oh, Great One?" he asked in Smurfette's voice.

"Yes, lying, deceptive, horrible little Smurfette?" Gargamel responded.

Assuming her high-pitched voice, Gargamel answered himself. "After all these years of Smurfless searching, how did you manage to find us?"

"Oh, I'm very glad you asked, my dear. For, you see, I have a magic map." He turned and pointed to a poster tacked to the wall. Nearly every area around the castle and throughout the forest was blocked out with big Xs. All except one place. "Soon, you will be mine! I shall now use my formidable powers to magically transport us here. . . ."

Gargamel crossed the room and pointed to the blank spot on the map. "Where the Smurfroot grows."

"Meow," agreed the cat.

Anxious to go there immediately, Gargamel raised his sorcerer's wand. "Come, my little fish-breathed friend!" He motioned for Azrael to move closer. With a swipe of his wand toward the spot on the map, Gargamel chanted the magic word: "AlakaZOOM!"

BAAM!

When the dust settled and the explosion cleared,

Gargamel and Azrael found themselves stuck in a hole in the wall, embedded into the map—a far cry from the forest where they were supposed to land.

"Ugh. Great." Gargamel sighed. What good is being a sorcerer if you can't cast spells the right way?

"Meow," complained Azrael.

"Yes, I can see that." Gargamel readied his wand to try again. "We really need that Smurf essence." He cast a second spell. "Ala-ka-zah!"

This time Gargamel's spell blew off his castle's roof.

"Aaaaaagh!!!" the wizard and the cat screamed together as they scrambled away from the falling debris.

Once the dust settled, Gargamel would try another spell. And another. He would not give up until he found those Smurfs!

Chapter 4

"Once every three hundred and sixty-five days, a Blue Moon rises that infuses the Smurf world with magic, love, and blueness."

Narrator reported from outside Papa's mushroom house. He walked up to Papa's window, peeked inside, then continued speaking to his TV camera. "During this time Papa Smurf is able to summon a vision of the future. It's really pretty cool!"

Inside, Papa was hard at work in his laboratory. Nestled among his library of alchemy books, cubbies filled with gear, and shelves of ingredients in storage containers, a steel cauldron sat atop a raging fire. White steam rose from the boiling potion.

"Hair of the dog that bit me," Papa said to himself as he reviewed the recipe. "And the last of my Smurfroot."

"I must get the visioning potion just right for the festival." Papa tossed the Smurfroot into the cauldron. "The magic is always strongest during the Blue Moon."

A fuzzy haze appeared over the cauldron. In the white shimmering smoke a vision appeared. Smurfs smiling.

Singing and dancing. Baskets full of Smurfberries.

"So far, so good," Papa said. "Lots of smiles and Smurfberries, Clumsy sitting still. That's always good—"

BOOM! Suddenly an explosion rocked the pot. Black shadowy smoke exploded out of the potion.

"What? What's happening?" he exclaimed, stepping back, horrified, as dark visions appeared in the shadows.

It began with a sinister hand holding a dragon wand. Then there was a grainy image of Clumsy diving to catch something. "I got it! I got it!" But no. Clumsy missed whatever it was. It hit his hand and bounced away.

"Clumsy." The name came out as a whisper. Papa trembled with fear. He knew he was seeing a forecast of the future.

Then the vision changed. Now a wispy gray medieval castle rose from the cauldron. Papa could see a dank and creepy dungeon filled with chilling machinery. Papa's eyes grew wide as he noticed that behind the machinery, all the Smurfs were locked in cages. They looked terrified—

"Help! Papa! Papa, save us! Help us! Papa! Papa!" Smurfs called out to Papa from the vision.

Papa's eyes grew wide. "Oh Clumsy," Papa moaned. "What have you done?"

The door to Papa Smurf's mushroom opened and a draft of cool air rushed in. The smoke quickly disappeared, taking the gruesome vision along with it.

"Hey, Papa."

"Clumsy," Papa greeted his visitor in a shaky voice.

"Are you okay?" Clumsy asked.

Papa turned his face toward the wall and willed his fear to go away. "Yes," he told Clumsy. "Fine. Why aren't you rehearsing for the Blue Moon celebration?"

"Oh, you know, a couple guys got smacked in the face," Clumsy replied casually. "So I thought I'd make some Smurfroot mudpacks to . . . um . . . take down everyone's swelling." As he said it, Clumsy crossed the laboratory to search through Papa's shelves of ingredients.

"Papa, you're smurf out of Smurfroot," Clumsy said. Papa Smurf was rereading the visioning recipe with a frown. "I'll go pick some," Clumsy told him.

When Papa looked up, the entire vision came back in a flash. Castle, dungeon, creepy cages. Captured Smurfs!

"No!" Papa shouted, snatching the empty Smurfroot container out of Clumsy's hands. "Those fields are too close to Gargamel's castle," Papa warned. "I'll get the Smurfroot. You stay in the village and out of trouble." Papa gave Clumsy a look that meant he was very, very serious. "Do you understand?" he asked.

Clumsy sighed.

Papa took that as a yes and returned to his potion. "Just . . . let me finish here first."

"Okay, if you say so," Clumsy agreed before leaving Papa to do his work.

Still inside his laboratory, Papa considered what he'd seen in the visioning potion. "The vision has never been wrong. I can't let this happen to my Smurfs." But was there anything he could do to change the future?

A short time later, Clumsy was out in the forest, doing exactly what he'd been told not to do—picking Smurfroot.

"Just stay in the village, Clumsy." Clumsy was talking to himself, imitating Papa's worried voice.

Looking around, he smiled. "Ha! Look at all this Smurfroot. They are going to be so proud of me."

Clumsy put a few fresh roots in a sack.

"Let's see, just a few more." Clumsy was about to pick a thick root when he noticed the tall grass behind him rattle and shake. Clumsy turned to see what was going on.

A cat's nose poked out through the bushes.

Clumsy knew that cat! It was Azrael . . . ready to pounce.

Right behind the feline, the cat's owner was headed Clumsy's way, carrying a Smurf-size net.

"G-g-g-g!" Clumsy cried out.

"Boo!" the wizard spooked Clumsy.

"Gargamel!" Clumsy dropped the piece of root, grabbed his sack, and ran.

Sprinting through the woods, Clumsy dashed around trees and over rocks. But everywhere Clumsy went, the cat was right behind, swiping his paw and just barely missing Clumsy's head with his sharpened claws.

Clumsy tried to distract Azrael. "Good kitty, good kitty! Look, look! A ball of yarn and a nice juicy bird!"

But Azrael kept on coming.

Clumsy was out of breath and exhausted. He couldn't

find anywhere to hide. There was only one thing to do. . . .

Clumsy saved himself by running straight through the invisibility shield, taking cover in the safety of Smurf Village.

Gargamel watched as the Smurf disappeared into thin air. One second he was in the clearing and the next . . . *POOF!* The little blue creature had vanished!

"So that's it!" Gargamel cheered as he realized what he'd seen. "It's invisible!" After all the years of searching, he finally understood why he'd never found Smurf Village before. "Oh, those sneaky little—"

"Meow," Azrael agreed.

Gargamel swooped his cat up and gave him a happy hug.

"Wait," he said. Gargamel glanced from the invisibility shield to Azrael and then back. "We don't know if it's safe."

There was only one way to find out. The look on the wizard's face was perfectly sinister as he tossed Azrael through the invisibility shield.

The cat vanished. A loud thud came from the other side.

"Azrael?" Gargamel leaned in close to the place where his cat had disappeared. "Are you dead?"

"Merowwww!"

Not dead.

"Ah!" Gargamel exclaimed, rubbing his hands together. Infinite power was finally within his grasp. Once he'd captured the Smurfs and drained them of their blue essence, Gargamel would truly be invincible!

Chapter 5

Back at Papa's mushroom, a couple of Smurfs were preparing to carry his magical cauldron into town for the festival.

"So, what did you see in your vision, Papa?" Smurfette asked. Her voice was filled with excitement.

Papa wasn't sure how to reply. He didn't want to scare Smurfette. "Oh, um, nothing apocalyptic, really. Everything is going to be just fine."

"Perfect!" Smurfette said happily. "Another year we don't have to worry about that mean ol'—"

"GARGAMEL!!!" Clumsy Smurf screeched at the top of his lungs as he ran by.

"I knew who she meant, Clumsy," Papa called after him.

Clumsy could barely breathe, he was so frightened. "No, NO! GARGAMEL!!!" He pointed a trembling finger toward the trees. "I mighta, kinda, sorta, accidentally led him to the village."

Papa and Smurfette were stunned to see the gigantic wizard charging toward them with his net.

"Hello, Smurfs." Gargamel stomped his big feet through

town, crushing everything in his path. He laughed loudly in an evil wizard's cackle.

"Smurf for your lives!" Vanity shouted as he dashed by at top speed.

"Everybody, skedaddle!" Handy advised, following Vanity.

Baker was worried. "Oh no! My cupcakes!"

Azrael sat down on top of a mushroom house, watching the Smurfs scatter around him.

It was chaos. Seeing no other alternative, Papa declared, "Into the forest, Smurfs!"

Smurfette grabbed Clumsy's arm. "Come on, Clumsy!"

"Sound the alarm, Crazy!" Papa Smurf instructed.

"BRRINNNGG! BRRINNGG!" Crazy Smurf began to call out.

"Head for the hills!" Farmer announced. The Smurfs began to run—left and right, forward and backward—in every direction all at once.

"This is bad! This is *really* bad!" one Smurf declared before he ran away.

"Save the schnitzel!" Chef yelled, making a beeline for his kitchen.

While Gargamel stood in the center of town, giddy with joy, Gutsy tried to distract Azrael, giving the other Smurfs a little extra time to run away. He got the cat's attention, then started to run.

"Azrael, over here. Come on," Gutsy called to him, jogging wildly through town with the cat hot on his heels. Finally Gutsy flung himself through the open window of a mushroom house. Azrael followed, but when the cat tried to see where Gutsy had gone, his big furry head got stuck in the small window.

Gutsy was proud of his own work. "Da, there you go, you nasty cat."

Azrael swiped his claw at the Smurf but could not reach him.

Before joining the others in the forest, Papa rushed back to his cottage. But just as he reached his home, Gargamel stepped on it, crushing the mushroom to pieces.

Papa tumbled backward.

"Papa." Gargamel stared menacingly at the older Smurf and raised his net.

When the net swooped down, Papa barely escaped being captured.

Gargamel swung his net again, desperately trying to scoop up Papa Smurf, but this time he caught a tree instead.

While Gargamel untangled his net from the tree, Papa went inside the ruined remains of his mushroom home. In the wreckage, he surprisingly managed to find what he had returned for inside a locked cabinet. On the front of the cabinet, it read: IN CASE OF EMERGENCY BREAK GLASS. Papa smashed the glass and pulled out a leather pouch of precious Smurfberries. Then Papa Smurf began to run with the others.

"Let go, cursed nature!" Gargamel finally freed his net from the tree branch and leaped toward Papa. "Here comes Papa, Papa!"

Papa dove out of the way in the nick of time. Zipping

past the net, Papa cut a nearby vine, causing a booby-trapped log to come swooping down, aimed directly at Gargamel's head.

Gargamel stopped short and the log swung by, narrowly missing him.

"Ha-ha, Papa!" Gargamel chuckled. "Your primitive defenses are useless against me. I laugh at them. Ha-ha. Hey—"

The log that had passed Gargamel a few seconds before was still swinging. It went up and up until it hit a big boulder. That rock fell loosely onto a switch that released a spring, sending a larger, much thicker log back. That log smacked Gargamel in the head.

WHAM! The log bowled him over, knocking Gargamel to the ground.

"How's that for primitive, Gargamel?" Papa asked, cracking a satisfied grin.

With Azrael and Gargamel temporarily stalled, the Smurfs got a head start into the forest. Clumsy was ahead of the pack. When he reached a fork in the road, he didn't know which way to go. The sun was setting and the light was becoming thin. He could see that the path to the right curved into the forest. To the left, the leaf-covered road led to a large-mouthed grotto.

"Maybe this will all blow over. Oh, yeah, I'm sure I can fix this. I just gotta think." Clumsy chose to go left, following a sign half-covered with leaves that read, GO THIS WAY.

"Yes! Follow me, everyone!" Clumsy hurried down the path.

A few minutes later, when the other Smurfs arrived at the same sign, some of the leaves had blown off, revealing what Clumsy unfortunately had missed. The sign actually read: DO NOT GO THIS WAY!

"Save yourselves!" Farmer shouted. He followed the other fleeing Smurfs to the right, farther into the forest.

But Smurfette saw Clumsy and knew he was going the wrong way. She could tell that he was rushing past the warning signs without reading them. They read: FORBIDDEN GROTTO, CERTAIN DEATH, and WE MEAN IT!

"Clumsy!" Smurfette called out to him. "You're going the wrong way!"

Just then Papa came running up with Grouchy, Brainy, and Gutsy.

"He's heading for the Forbidden Falls!" Brainy pointed down the path.

Grouchy moaned. "With the Blue Moon coming?"

"Quickly, Smurfs," Papa said urgently. "Stop him."

Smurfette, Brainy, Grouchy, Gutsy, and Papa hurried after Clumsy.

"Unbelievable!" Gutsy cried out, shocked by what he was seeing! "The one time we want him to trip and he's running perfectly."

"CLUMSY!" Grouchy called out, but Clumsy didn't stop.

Brainy shook his head. "Oh, this is a predicament."

The posted warnings were getting more and more frightening. Grouchy read one out loud as they passed it: AGONY AHEAD. He turned to the group. "Anybody reading these signs?"

Lost for words, Brainy could only repeat his previous sentiment. "This is a predicament."

"This guy's killing me," Grouchy complained, following along after the others.

"Come back here, Clumsy!" Gutsy called out, but Clumsy kept on going, running hard as if Azrael was still clawing at his heels.

At the entrance to the forbidden grotto, Papa, Smurfette, Brainy, Gutsy, and Grouchy paused, considering what to do.

"Looks like we're down to ninety-eight Smurfs," Grouchy said with a sigh.

And yet, they all followed Clumsy, stepping gingerly into the dank, dark cave.

Clumsy was hurrying along when suddenly the path ended. Directly in front of him there was a huge waterfall. If Clumsy hadn't stopped so fast, he would have surely fallen over the high cliff. As it was, he teetered on the edge.

"CLUMSY!"

Hearing his name, Clumsy turned to see who was calling and, in the process, lost his balance. He slid over the side of the sheer rock wall.

The Smurfs caught up then and peered over the cliff.

Shaking his head, Grouchy turned to leave. "Oh. Well, we tried, let's go."

"Help!" Clumsy was hanging onto a dangling root, his blue knuckles turning bluer.

"Hold on, lad!" Gutsy called. "We'll form a Smurf bridge to git ya!"

"Not the Smurf bridge." Grouchy rolled his eyes right back at Gutsy.

The Smurfs linked arms. Reluctantly, Grouchy agreed to be part of the rescue.

When they'd made a chain, Gutsy scooted closer and closer to the edge, his free hand stretched out toward Clumsy.

"Pardon me, but this is not a Smurf bridge," Brainy commented. "It's clearly a—"

"Smurf it, Brainy!" they all said together, cutting him off.

Just then the clouds parted.

Smurfette looked up at the clear evening sky. "Whoa!" She gasped. "The Blue Moon!"

"Oh dear," Grouchy said.

When the light of the moon hit the waterfall, a misty, swirling hole began to magically expand in the cascading water.

"What's happening, Papa?" Smurfette wanted to know.

Gutsy was also curious. "What the blinkin' flip is that?"

"Oh no." From the vision in the cauldron, Papa Smurf knew exactly what was going on. But there was no time to explain. They had to save Clumsy and get out of there. Now!

The hole was sucking Clumsy down. "Help!" he cried, struggling to hang on to the slippery root.

"Pull him up! Pull him up!" Gutsy told the others.

The Smurfs reached out, but no matter how hard they tried, they couldn't get to Clumsy.

Farther and farther they stretched. Closer and closer.

But Clumsy couldn't hold on any longer. His grip slipped. . . .

And then Clumsy disappeared into the hole.

The rest of the Smurfs fought hard to keep their footing, but the hole was dragging them in too. One by one they skidded off the stable ground, dangling over the waterfall below. Hanging in midair, they formed like a horizontal line of Smurfs.

"Whoa! Look out for the hole!" Grouchy saw that the thing was expanding.

Brainy couldn't help but correct, "It's more of a vortex or a portal."

Grouchy replied, "Smurf up! It's a hole."

"Hold on!" Smurfette yelled to them all. The hole tugged on them with a mighty power.

Papa was the last Smurf on solid ground. As he was being dragged off the cliff's edge, he grabbed hold of a stick. The wooden branch felt firm and solid—

Papa looked up only to find that the other end was being held by Gargamel.

"Seems you've got the short end of the stick, eh, Papa?" Gargamel joked.

Papa checked all around the grotto. Azrael hissed at the blue creatures. There was no escape.

Gargamel began to lift the chain of Smurfs up, away from the vortex. "Now you belong to me," Gargamel said with certainty.

"Not this time, Gargamel." Papa took a large gulping breath, then let go of Gargamel's stick.

Papa, Smurfette, Brainy, Grouchy, and Gutsy were immediately sucked into the vortex.

"No! Nooo!" Gargamel bellowed as the last Smurfy blue head vanished from sight.

Chapter 6

After a dark and windy journey, six screaming Smurfs crash-landed on a grassy area near a giant waterfall.

Grouchy was at the bottom of the Smurf pileup. "What's wrong with you?" he asked Gutsy, who had a huge smile stretching across his face.

"That . . . was . . . grrreat!" Gutsy roared. "Let's have another go!"

"Are you smurfed?" Grouchy couldn't believe his ears. "We nearly died in there!"

Smurfette checked her clothing. "We're not even wet."

Brainy surveyed the area. The waterfall they were standing behind seemed similar to the one in the grotto and so did the nearby pond. Similar, but not the same. "What part of the enchanted forest is this? My calculations indicate that—"

WHACK!

A slice of pizza hit Brainy. The cheese stuck to his head as tomato sauce dripped down the side of his face. He wiped cheesy grease off his forehead. "Ugh. That's slimy." Brainy then took a good look around. They were in an area overflowing with trashcans.

"I don't think we are in Smurf Village anymore," Smurfette remarked.

"Uh . . . Smurfs?" Clumsy called out to them. He was standing nearby, on top of a large rock. "You may want to take a look at this."

Gutsy was the first to head over. "What is it?"

Papa followed Gutsy up the rock. He was worried because he hadn't yet found a way to stop the terrible vision from coming true.

"Why are we listening to Clumsy?" Grouchy mumbled. "He just got us sucked through a giant hole."

Brainy put his hands on his hips and insisted, "It's not a hole. It's a vortex." Having provided the proper word, Brainy began to climb the boulder.

Grouchy sighed. "Can't we just go around the rock?" And then, when no one replied, he pulled himself up alongside the others.

When Smurfette reached the place Clumsy was standing, her eyes grew wide. She couldn't believe what she saw! All around them were towering buildings made of steel and glass. The loud honking sounds of cars and buses. People and traffic and the crazy mix of different smells.

"Oh. My. Smurf." Smurfette gasped.

"Where the smurf are we?" Grouchy grumped.

"Up the smurfin' creek without a paddle, that's where," Gutsy replied, pointing to the portal in the waterfall. It was closing!

"Well, at least they're not coming after us," Brainy said, referring to Gargamel and Azrael.

"Oh, yeah, relief," Grouchy said sarcastically.

But just then, Azrael shot through the portal and landed with a solid *THUMP!*

"Azrael!" Clumsy cried out.

Without any hesitation, Papa commanded everyone to run. Together, they all began to dash through New York City's Central Park.

Gargamel, who was still standing in the forest grotto, shouted into the hole for his cat. "Azrael? Are you dead?"

No reply.

Gargamel looked at the sky. Clouds were gathering over the Blue Moon, and the portal was beginning to shrink. He had little choice.

"Must. Have. Smurfs."

And so, Gargamel jumped.

The Smurfs continued to run away from the waterfall, unsure where they were headed, or if they'd ever make it back to Smurf Village again.

Papa tried to reassure them. "We'll circle back," he said calmly, "when it's safe." Papa wanted to keep moving. Azrael was out there, and they couldn't afford to stay in one place for too long.

"Guys, come on!" Smurfette encouraged everyone to stay together.

"Go!" Gutsy said, in full agreement.

"Comin' through!" Brainy was ready to hustle. He didn't want to see that cat again. Ever.

Only Grouchy was lagging behind. He'd had enough running for one day. "I'm getting hungry," he complained, as he and the rest of the Smurfs ran away from the waterfall and in the direction of a large boathouse.

Inside, the boathouse bash—which was hosted by Anjelou Cosmetics—was in full swing. Reporters and photographers were eating hors d'oeuvres, drinking, and talking endlessly about the newest product. It was called Jouvenel, and the company claimed it was like owning the Fountain of Youth in an Anjelou bottle. In just a couple of days, the cream would be for sale at stores all over the world.

Patrick Winslow greeted each and every person at the event. As a marketing employee at Anjelou, he knew if the reporters were happy, they would say nice things. So far, so good.

"Hey, can we get the photographer over there?" Patrick asked an Anjelou assistant, pointing to a group of nicely dressed men and women who were just about to enter the room. "There are big arrivals happening. Thanks."

The assistant rushed off and Patrick went to get himself a drink. On his way, Patrick noticed two frowning Anjelou models standing by a Jouvenel display.

"Hey, ladies," Patrick greeted them. "Lookin' good. Just a couple quick tips." He moved one of the girls. "If you could not stand directly in front of the display, but over to the side, it would be a bit more visible." He then positioned the second girl. "Hey, look, product!" he said as the display came into clear view.

"And don't forget to smile. Remember, you're working for a cosmetics company. That's it. Smile, relax, everyone will have a good time. Thanks. Thank you so much."

When the models were in place and grinning, Patrick moved on. Momentarily, Ms. Jouvenel's assistant, Henri, appeared at his side.

"Hello, Henri," Patrick said.

"On top of everything with the campaign, Patrick?" Henri asked.

"As much as I can be," Patrick replied. "We certainly did our homework, and tested the results." He shrugged. There wasn't much more he could do to make this launch successful.

"Patrick!" Just then Odile Jouvenel, the company owner, called to him from across the room.

The press loved Odile because she was successful, young, beautiful, and spoke with a charming Spanish accent. To those who worked for her, however, she was tough, demanding, and unpredictably impulsive.

Patrick looked at Odile and shivered. "She's pointing at me."

"That can't be good," Henri told him, clicking his tongue and shaking his head.

Patrick knew Henri was right. Nervously, he headed over to see what Odile wanted.

"Odile, it looks fantastic for Thursday's launch," a reporter gushed.

Odile replied, "It's going to be *quite* the gala."

They all shared a show-bizzy laugh as Patrick joined Odile and the circle of her admirers.

"Ah, there he is," she told them. "My new vice president of marketing." The reporters congratulated Patrick before moving on.

"You . . . fired Ralph?" Patrick stammered. He was shocked.

Odile casually shrugged. "His campaign was rubbish. He gave me what I asked for, not what I wanted. Can you give me what I *want*?"

"Is that what you're *asking* for?" Patrick replied, uncertain what she meant.

"How would I know what I'm *asking* for when I don't know what I *want*?" Odile countered.

"Well said, Odile. Well said." Patrick let Odile's words sink in. "Which is why you need me."

Odile smiled. "*Exacto*. I need you to create a new campaign for Jouvenel. All digital, of course, so it can be ready in time for the launch."

Patrick couldn't help but remind her, "Odile, that's in two days."

"Si, mi corazon," Odile put her hand on Patrick's arm. "And it mustn't be delayed. Will that be a problem?"

"Uh . . . no. No. I mean, I'll have to miss my wife's first ultrasound appointment—"

At thirty-five years of age, Patrick never expected to be the vice president of anything. He was having trouble wrapping his head around this huge promotion and the work it would take to make an entirely new advertising campaign by Thursday!

Odile gave him a disappointed look.

Patrick regrouped. "Two days is *perfect*. I mean, God only needed six days for the whole world, right?"

Odile tightened her grip around Patrick's arm like a vice. "Fail me and maybe you can go work for Him." Odile let go and stalked off.

Henri appeared at Patrick's side. "So? How'd it go?"

Patrick answered hurriedly. "Fine. Good. Great. A little out of my comfort zone but nothing I can't handle."

His words sounded confident, but inside Patrick was uncertain. He rushed to gather his things. If he was going to remake an entire advertising campaign in two days, he was going to have to get started immediately!

Arriving through the vortex, Gargamel splashed down in the Central Park pond. He wrung water out of his robes as he took in the scene. People were everywhere enjoying the sunny New York day. There were in-line skaters carrying boom boxes blaring hip-hop tunes, street performers, and even a family riding along on Segways.

"What manner of freakish realm is this?" he muttered.

"Meow," was Azrael's reply.

Gargamel went for a walk, both to explore and to search for the Smurfs. Azrael stayed where he was, stalking around the portal area where they'd all landed.

With the help of an Anjelou assistant, Patrick left the boathouse with heavy boxes full of files in tow. The assistant stacked the boxes on a park bench, while Patrick went back into the boathouse to get one more box.

"Can you grab a cab for me?" he called out to the assistant on his way back inside.

Just then the Smurfs arrived at the boathouse.

"This day keeps getting better and better," Grouchy whined.

"So," began Clumsy, checking around to make sure they had successfully ditched Azrael. "We're just going to jump in the portal, get back to our village, and everybody's happy, right?"

Papa nodded and they turned around, starting back around the lake, toward the portal.

Always the cheerleader, Smurfette tried to lift everyone's spirits. "Yeah, guys, let's stay smurftamistic."

Grouchy wasn't buying it. "You know what? I choose to be pessi-smurfistic. We're all going to die," he groaned.

When they reached the portal area, Brainy had a question. A big question. "Um, Papa?" Brainy began. "How do we get home with the portal closed?" Brainy pointed to the vortex spot. The hole was, in fact, now completely gone!

Papa didn't know what to say, but he didn't want to alarm the others. So he told them the answer he hoped in his heart was true. "I'm sure the Blue Moon will rise here tonight, the portal will open, and we'll be back safe and sound in the village, with our whole family together again."

"I can't wait," Smurfette exclaimed excitedly.

"Yeah," Clumsy said, thinking about going home. "I miss them already."

But until the portal opened, they needed a place to hide.

"All right, let's take shelter until dark," Papa said.

"Aye, let's get smurfin'," Gutsy said.

"Okay, but I'm not happy," Grouchy chimed in.

Before any Smurf could utter another word, they were interrupted by a loud, "Meooooww!"

Azrael pounced, catching nothing but air.

The Smurfs scattered. Again.

"Guys, come on! This way!" Smurfette called out.

"To the trees!" Gutsy charged.

Discovering an escape route, Brainy cried out, "To the left! Up, up, up!"

"Move it, hurry!" Gutsy said.

Azrael chased the Smurfs up the tree.

The cat leaped up to bite Smurfette, but he missed, catching instead only a clump of her hair in his mouth.

"Smurfette!" Papa called out, worriedly.

"Owww!" Smurfette shrieked. "My hair! Get back, cat!"

The cat swallowed the clump with a distasteful gulp, then was immediately walloped on the nose by Smurfette's high heel.

Azrael recoiled, rubbing his hurt nose with his paw.

"Way to go, Smurfette," Clumsy said, sharing the victory. Smurfette's blow to Azrael gave the Smurfs time to gain some distance. Clumsy needed it the most—he still hadn't begun to climb the tree yet.

Hurt, but not ready to quit, Azrael turned to the source of that last, small Smurf voice. Azrael arched his back and hissed.

"Oh no!" Clumsy exclaimed. To save himself, he ran as fast as he could back toward the boathouse where they had been safe earlier.

When he reached the boathouse, Clumsy climbed a park bench in an effort to get away from the dangerous furball.

"Take one for the team, Clumsy!" Grouchy called out.

Clumsy ducked as Azrael charged, teeth bared, sharp claws scratching.

"Help!" Clumsy was climbing the rails of the bench as fast as he could. He safely reached the top of the seat, but then fell backward—right into one of Patrick's cardboard boxes.

"Oh Clumsy," Gutsy remarked, not really surprised at what happened.

The Smurfs gasped as Azrael crept closer and closer to the cornered Smurf.

"Clumsy!" Smurfette shouted from her perch in the tree.

But there wasn't anything they could do from up in the tree. Clumsy was out there, in danger, on his own.

Azrael was just about to scoop Clumsy up with his paw when Patrick came out of the boathouse and suddenly picked up the stack of boxes, including the one that held Clumsy. The Smurfs watched as the boxes were placed into the trunk of a waiting taxicab. Patrick hopped in, waved good-bye to the assistant, and the taxi started to pull away from the curb.

"Quickly, to the mechanical wagon," Papa Smurf said, dashing along the tree branch, following the taxi's path.

"Come on, Smurfs," Gutsy said, keeping pace.

"Why don't we just go around the tree?" Grouchy moaned when the Smurfs jumped from that tree to another, much bigger, one. Climbing one thick trunk had been hard enough!

But Grouchy caught up, and together, the five little Smurfs skirted through tree branches, following their klutzy blue friend.

Frustrated at his own fruitless Smurf search, Gargamel found his cat sitting on top of a trashcan, watching a taxi enter the lanes of traffic.

"There you are! By all means, relax and enjoy the fresh

air and the sunshine while my missing Smurfs could be anywhere!" Gargamel reprimanded, shaking his fist at Azrael.

With a hiss, Azrael glared at the departing taxi, hoping Gargamel would get his hint and follow the car with Clumsy inside it.

But Gargamel didn't understand.

With a second hiss, Azrael stared up at the wizard, trying to get the message across.

Azrael yowled, "Meow!"

"What?" Gargamel asked. "Where?"

Following Azrael's gaze down the street, Gargamel spotted his Smurfs running across the tree branch above, trying to chase the taxi. A crooked smile appeared across his face.

Seated inside the moving vehicle, Patrick gave the driver directions to his apartment building. "Seventh Street between First and A, please." The driver nodded and the cab gained speed.

Chapter 7

In the trees above, the Smurfs struggled to keep up with Clumsy's ride.

"Come on! Try to stay with me, Smurfs!" Gutsy directed, keeping his eyes glued to the taxi. Gutsy slid down a tree branch and walked, like a tightrope circus performer, across some scaffolding. The Smurfs all followed.

Grouchy complained. "I'm getting too old for this."

"Oh, slow down!" Brainy cried, unable to go as fast as the others. He tripped and nearly fell.

"Be careful, Brainy," Papa warned, helping Brainy get his footing. Then Papa and Smurfette rushed along the scaffolding, desperate to keep pace with the cab.

Gargamel and Azrael had begun chasing down the cab on foot. "Come back here with my Smurf!" Gargamel shouted at the taxi driver.

But the driver didn't even notice.

High on the scaffolding, the Smurfs were on the taxi's tail, about to jump off the tightrope-like metal, and onto the moving vehicle.

"Come on, Smurfs!" Gutsy encouraged.

"Don't look down," Papa warned.

"Hurry!" Smurfette told the others.

Brainy wasn't feeling too steady. "A jump from this height will knock the blue out of . . . Aaaagh!!!"

The Smurfs ahead of him mustered all of their courage and leaped from the scaffolding to the roof of the moving cab. Shoving aside his fears, Brainy jumped too.

The landing was rough.

"Oh, my hip!" Papa rubbed his old, aching bones.

Gargamel, still chasing the cab, saw the little blue creatures land on top of the taxi. "Smurfs!" He was ever so happy they were together now. Easier to catch them all!

"Gargamel!" Smurfette shouted and pointed at the wizard.

"Oh no," Grouchy said with a moan.

"Oh dear." Even Gutsy was concerned.

Gargamel ran faster, taking longer and quicker steps. "Stop that carriage!" he shouted to people on the street.

Grouchy pounded his fist on top of the cab, encouraging the driver to zoom faster. "Let's go, let's go!"

Inside the cab, Patrick reached into his pocket in search of his cell phone. It was empty. "Wait, wait, wait," he told the cab driver. "I forgot my phone."

The driver slammed on the brakes, stopping short so quickly that Gargamel, who was in hot pursuit of the car, slammed right into its rear window! The wizard crumpled to the ground.

Fortunately, the Smurfs were able to stand their ground on the top of the car.

"Never mind," Patrick told the driver, having located the phone in his other pocket. "Here it is." The cab once more started out toward Patrick's address: Seventh Street between First Avenue and Avenue A.

The Smurfs laughed as the taxi moved farther and farther away from Gargamel and his cat.

Grouchy yelled to the wizard, "Knock yourself off, Gargamel!"

Gutsy laughed the loudest. "You've had that coming for about thirty years."

Battered and bruised, Gargamel was furious that the Smurfs had escaped him yet again. But just as the wheels turned the corner, leaving the evil Gargamel behind, a small card broke free from the cab's bumper and fluttered toward him. It was a business card for a place called Anjelou Cosmetics. The wizard looked at the logo on the card. Could this be a clue?

Gargamel smiled. This Smurf-hunt wasn't over yet.

The Smurfs took in the sights of New York as the taxi rolled through Times Square.

"Oh wow!" Smurfette said. The others echoed her amazement. "Castles and palaces everywhere!"

By the side of the road, there was a street vendor dressed like the Statue of Liberty.

"Ooh, and green goblins!" Gutsy added, fascinated.

Another street vendor was dressed as clown.

"And red trolls," Smurfette noted.

Gutsy spotted a giant billboard. On it there was a picture of a beautiful woman wearing fancy clothing. "Ooh! And look at that giant princess!"

"Wow, this village is amazing, Papa!" Smurfette couldn't stop staring at the flashing billboards and buildings that seemed tall enough to reach the sky.

"Yes," Papa agreed. "And likely very dangerous. Until we rescue Clumsy and get back home, I need you all to stay close and do exactly as I say."

"Okay, Papa," Smurfette agreed. "If you say so."

"We promise," added Grouchy.

"Smurf's honor," vowed Brainy.

"Aye. You can count on us, Papa," Gutsy assured him.

Realizing they were out in the open, Brainy exclaimed, "Uh! Blend in!"

On top of the cab, there was an advertisement for a show called the Blue Man Group. The Smurfs leaned in close to the ad, looking exactly like the popular blue-colored entertainers. Feeling well hidden, they continued to take in the crazy sights of New York City.

Soon the taxi slowed in front of a brown building.

"I guess this is our stop. Let's go. . . ." Papa showed the others a nearby tree with a low-hanging branch.

"Yay! We get to climb another tree!" Smurfette said.

Grouchy moaned. "Yay."

Before the cab came to a complete stop, the Smurfs pulled themselves up and into the tree.

"Hang on, everybody, hang on! That's it!" Gutsy said as they all watched Patrick grab his boxes, exit the cab, and walk to the entrance of the building.

"Oh, I hope Clumsy can breathe in that box!" Smurfette said, concerned.

"How are we supposed to find Clumsy in there?" Grouchy groaned.

They all looked up at Patrick's apartment building. It was seven stories high and had lots and lots of windows on each floor.

Day was rapidly turning to night. Brainy studied the shadows on the building. "I could attempt to Smurf the probabilities—"

"Brainy!" Smurfette cut him off.

Papa had the easy solution. "We'll look through every window."

"I don't do windows," Grouchy argued.

No one paid any attention.

"Now, let's get smurfin'," Papa ordered, leading the way out of the tree and up to the first-level windows.

"Come on!" Gutsy followed.

Grouchy sighed. "Every window?"

Papa climbed the fire escape ladder.

Gutsy sized up the building. "Piece of cake," he announced confidently.

Grouchy muttered under his breath, "What's this guy smurfin'?"

Chapter 8

Patrick's wife, Grace, was sitting in the living room, relaxing in an armchair while softly reading a children's book to her pregnant belly. Nearby, a basset hound named Elway was sound asleep on the floor.

"Grace?!" Patrick came bounding into the room.

"Hello," Grace said, calmly setting down the book.

Patrick placed his boxes on the floor. "Guess what? Guess what? Guess what?"

"Ah, ah! Um, okay . . ." Grace thought about it, then teased, "They invented zero-calorie pizza."

"No, but that's a good idea."

One more try. "Yeah! Um, they found a—" Grace put a hand on her belly. "Oooh, the baby kicked!"

Patrick forgot his news for a minute. This was bigger. They were having a baby! "Ohh! Hi!" He kissed his wife.

Grace took Patrick's hand and set it on her belly. "Feel! Feel. Now, please say hello."

Patrick leaned in, not quite sure what to do. "Hello, little sea-monkey. This is, uh, this is the sound of my voice."

Grace giggled.

"Hello, son or daughter. Hello. Heelloo," Patrick continued.

Grace shook her head. "That's not your voice. That's a robot. Our child is going to get attached to the toaster."

"Or"—Patrick stood up, grinning gleefully—"the new VP of Marketing."

Grace popped out of her chair. "Get out!" She hugged her husband.

"Provisional," Patrick warned. "If I wow Cruella D'Odile, I keep the job. If I don't, my head probably goes on the pike next to the last guy's."

Grace was so happy. "And wow you will. You wowed me."

"Wowed. Wooed. Wed," Patrick said.

"Wombed." Grace added.

"Nice," Patrick complimented. "But I have two days," he continued, going back to talking about the job.

"Oh." Grace gasped. "Yikes."

"I know! What if I can't get it done in time?"

Grace suddenly realized what this meant. "Oh no. So you can't come to the ultrasound?"

"I don't know," Patrick answered honestly. "Unless . . . wait. The backup ads we have did fine in focus groups. I can retool those. I'd have to work around the clock. . . ."

As Patrick thought out his plan, Grace put on a brave smile to mask her disappointment.

Later that night Gargamel and Azrael were still in the now-quiet Central Park, sitting under a streetlight.

"Ah, Azrael," Gargamel said with a moan. "We've come so far, yet ever am I haunted by the same familiar riddle: *how* to find the Smurfs? If only I—"

Azrael began to cough, arching his back and making severe gagging noises.

Gargamel looked at the cat with disgust. "I'm sorry. Is my thinking interrupting your vile hacking?" He turned away from Azrael. "If only I had something of theirs, a drop of spittle, a fingernail . . ." Gargamel went on, "Some hair . . . even that would be enough to make some Smurf magic."

Azrael coughed harder. Finally, with a loud and nasty belch, he barfed up a hairball.

Gargamel turned up his nose at the horrid smell. "Very nice. Are you done now?"

"Meow."

"I don't want to look at it," Gargamel replied.

Azrael pushed the hairball across the cement with his small black nose.

"What? Blech. What?" Finally, with a gasp, Gargamel caught on. "Is that—no, it can't be. . . ." He picked up the hairball and held it in the faint light of the streetlamp. "It is!" he cheered. "The tawny locks of Smurfette!"

Realizing what a gem he held, Gargamel stuck his nose into the tangled, gooey mess. He took a deep sniff and said, "Oh, sweet follicular ambrosia! Oh, silky strands of joy." Then he couldn't help but gag. "Mixed with a fair amount of cat vomit."

Azrael gave a proud meow.

"Yes, Azrael, I *am* a genius!" Gargamel replied, shaking off some of the vomit from the hair. The gross puke hit Azrael in the eye. The cat rolled his watering eyes.

Ignoring this, Gargamel began looking around the park, squinting to see farther into the dark. "With my skills, this small trifle of Smurfiness will yield me just enough power to catch them all. I must find a laboratory in which to tease the magic from these precious strands."

Finally, Gargamel spotted a portable potty nearby. "Ooh, it's a bit small, but this should do nicely!" Gargamel and Azrael entered the potty. "Oh, look, it's even got its own cauldron."

That was when Gargamel took his first breath.

"Ugh, what died in this cauldron?!" he cried out. The stink was unbearable! "Open! Open!"

Gargamel tugged wildly at the door handle. When the potty door finally opened, Gargamel and Azrael stumbled out, gasping for fresh air. "Whoa. Someone's been working a dark and terrible magic in there," he said with a shiver.

Off in the distance, some outdoor lights popped on, illuminating a large, gray stone castle.

"Oooh. What is that?"

Gargamel hurried toward the lights of Central Park's historic Belvedere Castle and entered through the cellar doors. There he discovered a moldy, cluttered storage area in the basement.

He raised his hands in pure joy. "Oh baby! Daddy's home!"

Chapter 9

The Smurfs had looked in many, many windows. Clumsy was nowhere to be found. And they were exhausted! Still, they continued up the fire escape ladder, hopeful that they would find him soon.

Night had fallen and the full moon above was shining brightly. "Papa, I'm familiar with six hundred and thirteen shades of blue. That moon is not one of them." Brainy stared at the sky. "The full moon is decidedly white."

Papa nodded thoughtfully. "Stay calm, everyone. If the portal opened once, it can open again."

"How are we going to open a magical portal when we can't even find Clumsy?" Grouchy was losing his patience. He was so very tired.

Just then Gutsy called down from higher up on the fire escape. "Hey . . . I think I see something up here!" Something in a higher-level apartment caught his eye. "Clumsy, is that you?" he whispered to himself.

The Smurfs all scampered up to see for themselves.

Inside that apartment . . .

Clumsy was struggling to find a way out of the box in which he had traveled to this strange place. He pushed hard at the lid, only to find that his box was stationed right in the middle of a tall, heavy stack. The tower of cartons teetered as he tried to get free. After a few failed attempts, Clumsy gave the lid a gigantic shove. Stepping back to see what he'd done, Clumsy was relieved to find that he'd finally managed to force a hole large enough to escape through. On the lookout for any signs of danger, he nudged his head over the edge of the box and carefully peeked out.

There was no one around. It looked safe enough.

Clumsy pulled himself out and landed with a soft plop on the living room floor. He was surveying his surroundings when he noticed Patrick walking toward the door to the office.

"Huh?!" Clumsy nervously backed up—straight into a cold, wet dog nose!

"Augh!" Frightened, Clumsy ran. Elway tried to follow, but couldn't get enough traction on the wooden floors.

"Help! Heeeelp!" Luckily, Clumsy made it to the bathroom, where he immediately shut the door. Elway slammed his head into the closed door with a bang.

Clumsy had never before seen a room like the one he was in. The dog started pawing at the door as Clumsy scurried up the first thing he could grab hold of—the towel rack.

"Oh smurf!" Clumsy exclaimed excitedly, lowering himself off the rack and into the sink. Finally, a safe place to stand!

Feeling a bit calmer, he took a second to look around. His nose to led him to something sweet smelling, a nearby clear plastic container with a pump and a label that read: BUBBLE BOOM. Next to the words was a picture of berries.

"Berry . . . Boom . . . Mmmm." Hungry, Clumsy sucked down a mouthful.

BLECH! It was disgusting! Clumsy burped up a huge bubble that popped right smack in his face! Startled by the *POP!*, he fell back over the hair dryer, which accidentally turned on and blew him backward—*SPLASH!*—right into the toilet.

After a short rest, Clumsy attempted to climb out of the bowl and onto the seat using a dangling overhead chain for support when, uh-oh—*FLUSH!* He grabbed at the toilet paper roll to help halt his downward-spinning descent, but instead he found himself right back inside the toilet bowl, swirling around on a wad of soggy paper from the roll that continued to unfurl before his very eyes.

Outside the apartment, Gutsy showed the other Smurfs through the window. "I'm sure this is the box!" He told them, motioning to the cardboard box on the floor.

Grouchy peeked into the apartment. "When I get my hands on him—!"

The Smurfs entered through an open window and tiptoed over to the box tower. Brainy put a finger to his lips. "Shh! Someone's coming."

"Smurfs!" Papa whispered. He motioned for them all to duck and hide.

It was Grace. "Elway!" She called out. Having been awakened by Elway's clawing at the bathroom door, she finally got up to go see what all the fuss was about.

Hearing her milling around outside made the Smurfs move even more quickly. They had to get Clumsy out of that box before she came in and found them there! "Come on, put a little smurf into it!" Gutsy said, shoving at the cardboard.

"Hang on, Clumsy!" Smurfette said, hoping Clumsy could hear her from inside the box.

"Shhh, quiet!" Brainy warned again.

"All together now!" Papa put his fingers next to Smurfette's.

They climbed on top of Clumsy's box, and together they pried opened the lid. Ecstatic, they peered inside, frantically looking for Clumsy.

The box was filled to the brim with papers, but there was no sign of Clumsy.

Grouchy shook his head. "Ai, yi, yi."

"Now what, lads?" Gutsy asked.

Smurfette shrugged. "What happened to Clumsy?"

"I bet they ate him," Grouchy said. "Let's go home!"

Suddenly the sound and vibration of heavy footsteps

interrupted their search. Then the office door opened, and Patrick headed their way!

"Hide! Dive! Dive!" Papa Smurf told them.

All the Smurfs ducked low into the box, and Papa closed the lid over them. Whew! Just in time, because just then Patrick picked up that very box and carried it into his office.

Searching for some documents he needed, Patrick reached inside. Instead of finding papers, he discovered five little blue faces staring up at him.

"Ahhhh!" Patrick shouted in surprise.

"Ahhhh!" the Smurfs yelled back.

Outside the bathroom, Grace pushed Elway aside to see what was driving the dog mad. Entering the room, she found a roll of soggy toilet paper stuffed in the toilet.

"Elway, did you do that?" she asked the dog, lifting the mess out with the toilet brush.

She gave the dog a reprimanding tap on the nose then she started to toss the paper from the toilet into the trash bin. That's when the paper began to wiggle.

"Ahhhh!" Grace screamed, seeing Clumsy's little blue head poking out from the soggy clump of paper.

Clumsy shrieked back.

Scared witless, Grace panicked and flung Clumsy off the brush and against the windowsill, like a bug. Clumsy's shriek could be heard throughout the apartment. Even inside Patrick's office.

"That's Clumsy," Papa said worriedly, cupping his ear to listen through the box.

"Charge, Smurfs, charge!" Gutsy leaped out of the box and slammed into Patrick's leg. When Patrick fell to the ground, the Smurfs ran right over him toward the door.

"Clumsy," Smurfette shouted. "We're coming!"

On his way out Grouchy left Patrick with a little parting gift. "This is for Clumsy!" he growled, kicking Patrick just below the chin.

"Wait for me!" Brainy cried, trying to keep up.

Inside the bathroom Clumsy was cowering up against the windowsill. "Please don't hurt me! I just wanna go home."

"Are you . . . did you . . . did you just talk?" Grace asked, eyeing him suspiciously, the wet toilet brush dangling from one hand.

"I'm not saying till you put down the giant spiky thing!" he cried.

"Clumsy!" he heard Smurfette call out from the living room. "Where are you? Smurf us a sign!"

"Smurf out, smurf out, wherever you are!" another Smurf yelled.

"Can you hear us?" they shouted in unison.

Patrick peeled himself off the floor, grabbed an umbrella, and began chasing the Smurfs around the living room. Swinging wildly at their wee little heads, he tried desperately to force them toward the front door of the apartment.

"Get outta here!" he screamed, taking a swipe at Smurfette. "Back to the sewers."

Smurfette ducked.

Gutsy broke away from the group and scrambled up

the fireplace onto the mantle. "You lot, find Clumsy! The giant is mine!" Then he took a giant leap off of the mantle and crash-landed right on Patrick's back.

Patrick spun round and round, swinging his umbrella this way and that in an effort to pry the creature off his back. On his last swing he accidentally hit himself in the head! Exhausted and injured, he collapsed to the ground in a heap.

"Have you had enough? Tap out! Tap out!" Gutsy teased.

With Patrick distracted, Papa was able to scope out where Clumsy's voice was coming from. "Over here! Quickly!" he motioned for the other Smurfs to follow him.

Inside the bathroom, Grace was still in shock. "Okay, so you're like a . . . you're blue . . . and . . . oh!" She noticed that Clumsy was shivering from cold and fright. "Oh, gosh, are you okay?" she asked, genuinely concerned.

Hearing Grace, Grouchy got a better reading on where the voices were coming from. "This way, this way!" he directed.

"Clumsy, where are you?" Smurfette asked again, desperate to find her missing friend.

Hearing the Smurfs' voices in the hallway, Elway burst through the bathroom door and rushed into the hall to see who was out there, barking fiercely. Protective of Grace, he blocked their entrance to the restroom. Defeated, but only for the moment, the Smurfs retreated and ran back to the living room.

Elway chased them.

"Look out!" Brainy warned, seeing that Elway was quickly approaching.

Grouchy turned around. "Other way, other way!"

Patrick, who had just recovered after knocking himself out with the umbrella, stood up only to be accosted yet again by a chain of little blue creatures weaving circles around his legs, with Elway close behind.

"Run, Smurfs!" Gutsy said. Then he turned his attention to Elway. "You big, hairy, ugly cat!" he taunted from behind Patrick's leg. Elway launched himself at Gutsy.

"Elway!" Patrick shouted, but it was too late. The dog plowed into him, knocking him over—again.

Having finally bagged the giant, Gutsy began to lasso Patrick's hands together. "Stop bleatin' like a sheep an' let me hog-tie ya. Ya wrinkly numkin'."

Unable to move, he could only warn Grace when he spied the other Smurfs headed for the bathroom. "Grace! We're being attacked! Do not be tricked by their cuteness!"

"It's okay," Grace told him calmly, entering the living room carrying Clumsy lovingly in her arms. "They're friendly."

"Yer lucky yer lassie stepped in," Gutsy warned Patrick. "I was aboot to make haggis of yer innards."

Patrick took a long, hard look at the little blue creature by his side. Then he closed his tired eyes and wished that this was all just one, big, crazy dream.

Deep in the basement of Belvedere Castle, Gargamel was hard at work in his new laboratory. A candlelit flame burned below an old coffee urn, heating up a smoky substance. The vapor from the potion was being sucked through a long nozzle connected to an elaborate contraption. Gargamel held up a strand of Smurfette's hair. It glistened in the flickering candlelight.

"This is it, Azrael," Gargamel announced. "Smurfette's hair goes in here, through this Smurf essence extractor, and finally, I have my Smurfalator!" Gargamel clapped his hands. "Ha! It's the pièce de résistance, the crème de la—"

The wizard looked over and found that Azrael was too busy licking his own butt to listen.

Gargamel sighed. "If I could do that, I wouldn't care about Smurfs either."

Turning back to his machinery, with a flick of his wrist, he dropped the hair into the funnel-shaped top of the contraption. It began to whir as the engine kicked into action. Gargamel waited patiently. "Yesss. Yesss," he declared when a single drop of iridescent blue liquid gathered at the bottom of the spout. "With this precious elixir my spells will be powerful beyond all measurable . . . measurement!"

He captured the drop in his open signet ring and closed it tightly. The center stone glowed brightly, a nod to the incredible power that was housed inside.

Gargamel showed the ring to Azrael. "Ahh! This one tiny drop will give me the power to capture them all!" he exclaimed triumphantly.

His plan was finally falling into place. Soon enough he would have the Smurfs right where he wanted them. . . .

Chapter 10

"La, la la-la-la-la, sing a happy song . . ."

The next morning the Winslows' kitchen was full of merry Smurfs making their first human-style breakfast.

"Whoa, this is great!" Gutsy cried from atop the orange juicer. Clumsy held a glass to catch the sweet liquid.

Patrick, who was trying desperately to not be freaked out by the little blue creatures taking over his kitchen, poured himself a cup of coffee and a bowl of cereal, and sat down at the table with his laptop.

Grace laughed at her husband's stubborn attitude. Since the night before, he'd been insisting they were both dreaming.

While Patrick worked on an idea for Odile's campaign, Smurfette helped Grace wash strawberries in the sink.

"How crazy is this, Patrick?!" Grace burst out. "Little blue people! Singing in our kitchen!" An endearing grin spread across Grace's face.

On the counter, Grouchy was angrily stomping on the toaster pedal, trying to get the bread to pop up.

Brainy looked over at the toaster and laughed. "It's so obvious what you're doing wrong!"

"Oh really!" Grouchy asked, stepping aside to let Brainy have a try. "After you!"

"Clearly this mechanism works like this—" Brainy climbed onto the handle.

With a sinister laugh, Grouchy kicked the lever.

"Aaaaahhhh!" Brainy went soaring off the lever and did a face-plant directly into Patrick's cereal bowl.

Patrick wiped the table with a napkin. "So, you're sticking with your 'this is actually happening' theory?" Patrick asked his wife, shaking his head.

Grace just chuckled.

"Sorry," Brainy added, peeking out of the bowl, covered in milk and cereal.

But as skeptical as Patrick was, it was getting increasingly difficult to continue insisting that these blue guys didn't exist. Especially when one was swimming around in his cereal. So he decided to do some computer research.

"Okay, it says here, 'Smurfs are mythical creatures from Belgium.'" Patrick scrolled down. "'Also known as *Les Schtroumpfs*, documented by Peyo.'"

Grace crossed the kitchen to read over Patrick's shoulder. "Aww, it says they bring good luck. Like leprechauns to the Irish."

"It says they're *mythical*, Grace."

"Wooo-hooo!" One of the mythical creatures called out, flying across the kitchen. *SPLAT!* A giant spray of orange juice showered Patrick's laptop screen.

"I'm so sorry, Master Winslow," Papa apologized.

But Gutsy thought his dismount from the juicer had been quite a feat. "That was great!" he remarked.

"They look pretty real to me," Grace mused as Patrick wiped the spots of juice off of his screen. "Aw, look." She pointed at the dog, who was moaning happily while having his belly scratched by Clumsy.

Patrick didn't know what to believe. "Okay, to review: You guys come from a 'magic forest' where you live in oversize mushrooms."

"Yes," Papa confirmed.

"You're being chased by an evil wizard."

"Yeah," Papa said.

"And you're trapped in New York until there's a 'Blue Moon.'"

Papa was pleased. "Very good."

"And you like to use the extremely imprecise term 'smurf' for just about everything."

"Smurfxactly," Brainy affirmed.

Patrick raised his eyebrows in suspicion. "And you're all named after your personalities? Do you get your names when you're born or after you've exhibited certain traits?"

Papa climbed onto the table near Patrick's computer, eager to discuss a much more pressing matter. "Master Winslow," Papa began, with urgency in his voice. "Please, there must be *something* about the Blue Moon on your magic window machine."

"Whoa! Just what is this magic searching device?" Brainy wanted to know.

"Well, right now, I'm using a search engine," Patrick said.

"Ooooh," the Smurfs all cooed at the same time.

Patrick's fingers flew over the keys as he typed in a search: Blue Moon. "A full moon that occurs twice in one month . . . a figurative construct"—He couldn't help but add—"Much like yourselves."

"Hey!" Grouchy remarked, slightly offended.

Patrick rolled his eyes, then went on reading. "But the moon itself doesn't appear to be blue."

Hearing that, the Smurfs all stopped what they were doing and turned to stare at Papa.

"What?!" Brainy asked.

"Not blue?" Smurfette wondered.

"Oh perfect!" Grouchy whined.

"Now we'll never get home!" Gutsy exclaimed.

Papa leaped in front of the computer, both to stop Patrick from reading more and to hide the picture of the full moon in the center of the page.

"No cause for alarm, my little Smurfs," Papa reassured the others. He pinched his lips together thoughtfully. "If we're to open the portal home, I'll just have to smurf us a potion to invoke the Blue Moon."

Patrick turned to Grace. "You hear that, honey?" he began sarcastically. "They're only staying till the Blue Moon rises, which could happen if the little blue Santa man can make a magical potion." In a softer tone, he added, "Which at this point seems completely plausible."

Patrick reached out to grab the creamer for his coffee,

only to find Grouchy sitting on the lid of the creamer cup, eating a strawberry.

"Want a bite?" Grouchy asked.

Patrick shook his head. "No, thank you."

Papa continued thinking out loud. "Of course, the stars will need to be perfectly aligned. And when that might be is hard to determine without the proper instrument." Papa turned toward Patrick. "Master Winslow, might I borrow your Stargazer?"

"My what-whatzer?" Patrick didn't understand.

Gutsy knew immediately that this was a very bad sign. "Uh-oh. He doesn't have a Stargazer." He confirmed with Patrick, "Do ye?"

Patrick and Grace both shook their heads, still not fully comprehending.

"This is all my fault!" Clumsy wailed.

Brainy put his hands over his head and began sobbing. "We're all going to die! We're all going to die!" he cried.

Fearful this would lead to one big smurfy meltdown, Gutsy tried a little tough love with Brainy. "Smurf out of it, scaredybrains. One Panicky Smurf is enough!" he barked, shaking Brainy by the shoulders.

"Besides," Smurfette added calmly, "Papa had a vision and everything turns out smurfy. Right, Papa?"

They all turned to face Papa.

"Uh . . . yes, yes. It all turns out just . . . fine," Papa assured them.

But Papa's vision had been far from smurfy.

Chapter 11

"We must find this Smurf-thief!" Gargamel declared emphatically as he and Azrael stormed down a crowded New York City street.

Azrael hissed.

"Eh, stop your complaining," Gargamel shot back. Then, thinking, he added, "If I were a Smurf, where would I go?"

At that moment, a well-dressed businessman came hurrying down the street, chatting away on his Bluetooth earpiece.

"You there, Fancypants," Gargamel called out to him. "Have you seen any little blue men?"

The man, who hadn't paid Gargamel any attention, continued the conversation he was having with a telephone colleague over his wireless earpiece. "Absolutely, what price are we talking about?"

"You're selling them?" Gargamel asked, delightfully surprised.

Just then a young woman, also talking on her wireless earpiece, crossed the street right in front of Gargamel.

"Have you looked in the drawer, sweetie?"

Gargamel went after her. "What drawer?"

"In the kitchen, Lily," the woman replied.

"Lily? Who is this Lily?" Gargamel wondered aloud.

Just then a man wearing a plaid shirt and leather work boots answered his question: "Are you kidding me?" he told the person on the other end of his wireless earpiece. "She's like the hottest girl in my department."

Gargamel grabbed the man's arm, forcing him to stop. "Please, young woodsman. What does the temperature of this Lily have to do with finding the Smurfs?"

The guy yanked his arm away. "Take your meds, man!"

"What? Is everyone in this realm completely insane?" Gargamel asked his cat.

As he asked the question a homeless person bumped right into him. All the man's possessions were stuffed into a shopping cart.

"Ah, thank the gods—a local wizard. Excellent!" Gargamel exclaimed. "Pardon me, wise sir. By any chance have you seen any little blue men?"

The homeless person had a crazy look in his eyes. "They're everywhere!" he reported.

"I knew it! I told you we're close, Azrael," Gargamel said confidently to his pet.

The cat simply rolled his eyes.

In the Winslows' apartment, Papa gathered the Smurfs in the living room to hand out Smurfberries. "Now, take just one. We have to be careful to make sure our Smurfberries last."

"Great," Grouchy said ironically. Then he popped one in his mouth. "We're gonna be here how long?"

"Not long." Papa gave Smurfette her berry. "I have a plan. First we have to get a Stargazer. Next find a book of spells, and then smurf a portal and we're home. Very simple, my little Smurfs."

The second the Smurfs ate their berries, the color of their skin immediately improved to a richer, darker, healthier blue.

Papa put away the bag just as Patrick entered the living room, dressed for work.

"Oooh! Someone looks smurf-a-lish!" Smurfette cheered.

"Why are ya wearing a leash?" Gutsy wanted to know.

"It's a tie," Patrick replied, tugging the knot a little bit tighter.

"Does it keep your neck warm?" Grouchy wondered aloud.

"No, it's . . ." Patrick paused, having trouble finding the words to explain.

Brainy helped, thinking he had found the most logical reason. "Clearly it functions as an aid in his craft, like a blacksmith's apron."

"No. I wear it because . . . it's what *everyone* wears to work," Patrick said.

The Smurfs stared at him, confused.

Gutsy had another question. "What are ye, ya pasty giant?"

Patrick shook his head. "I try to get people to buy things by analyzing market trend predictions and—"

"Predictions!" Brainy exclaimed! *That* was a job he was familiar with. "Aha. He's a fortune-teller!"

With a deep breath, Patrick gave up. "Not exactly. Look, I would love to explain but I am superlate and I gotta go." He began gathering the things he needed to take to work.

Grace entered the room in a hurry too. She slipped on her shoes and rushed to put the finishing touches on her outfit.

Smurfette's eyes went wide. "What?! You had one outfit on, and now you're wearing something completely different!" She exclaimed with amazement.

Papa put his hand on Smurfette's shoulder. "Now, Smurfette," he said softly, "she probably got the other one dirty. Let's not embarrass her."

Smurfette nodded, glancing away from Grace. "Oh sorry," she said.

Clumsy climbed onto the table where Grace was searching for keys in her purse. "Thanks for letting us stay in your mushroom, Miss Grace. It's really nice!"

Grace grinned. "Why, thank you. I'm glad you like it. I love our little mushroom too." She turned her eyes toward Patrick and lowered her voice. "But *somebody* wants a bigger mushroom."

Smurfette was shocked. "But then you'd be farther apart!"

"You said it, sister." Grace laughed. "Okay. I've got to run to an appointment. We've got a baby on the way."

All the Smurfs smiled, but Smurfette's smile was the brightest.

Patrick turned to Grace. "We can't leave them here alone, without an adult," he implored.

Papa assured Patrick that they'd be fine on their own. "I'm five hundred and forty-six years old."

Patrick took a deep breath. "Of course you are," he finally replied.

Grace kissed her husband good-bye. "They'll be *fine*."

"Okay. Love you." Patrick gave Grace a quick kiss.

Grace waved at the Smurfs, then hurried out the door.

Snagging the computer off the table, Patrick also headed out. Before leaving, he turned back to the Smurfs. "By the way, I wouldn't go anywhere if I were you."

"Why not?" Smurfette asked.

"Our world doesn't do well with visitors from other places." Seeing that the Smurfs didn't get what he was implying, Patrick offered up an example. "I mean, look what happened to E.T." The Smurfs stared at him, jaws hung open. He continued, sure they'd recognize the character sooner or later. "*E.T.*? The movie? The moving picture? The book?"

Still nothing.

"Just stay, okay?" he concluded.

With that he shut the door to the apartment, leaving the Smurfs alone.

"Great," Grouchy said, flopping back into the sofa. "He's gone, and we still don't have a Stargazer."

"Wait a smurf!" Brainy just had a brilliant idea! "If he's a fortune-teller, he reads stars all the time! Ergo, it's at his place of business!"

Papa gave Brainy a pat on the back. "Excellent work, Brainy!"

Gutsy looked at Brainy with admiration. "What are we waiting for, a smurfitation? Let's ride!"

"Yeah! Come on, guys!" Clumsy added enthusiastically.

"Come on, Smurfs, to the window!" Gutsy advised.

Papa, too, was excited to find them a way home. "Let's go get that Stargazer!"

The Smurfs started out the window. Before he could even reach the sill, Clumsy tripped over his own feet and fell backward onto the couch. Everyone turned to stare at him. The fall had been a reminder of Clumsy's unstable feet, and the trouble they could cause in this dangerous, new realm.

Papa Smurf turned to the fallen Smurf. "Clumsy, I think it might be best if you, uh, if you stay here. You know, smurf an eye on the mushroom."

Papa was trying to be nice, suggesting that watching over the Winslows' mushroom was an equally important job. But Clumsy got the message loud and clear. "Yeah. That's what I was thinking," he answered bravely. Though inside he was hurting, he backed away from the window and took a seat on the couch.

"This way, Smurfs!" Gutsy called, directing everyone out the fire escape.

"Let's follow Mr. Winslow!" Papa announced, halfway out the window.

As Clumsy watched the others climb down the ladder one by one, he tried to encourage himself to stay upbeat. "Yeah," he reiterated, "I can smurf an eye on the mushroom!"

Gutsy was the last to jump out the window onto the fire escape. "Smurf a leg!" he called down to his fellow Smurfs who had gotten a head start.

Brainy looked over the edge. "Can you see him? Is he down there?" he asked.

Far below, at street level, Gutsy spotted Patrick standing at the curb, piling his boxes into a taxi. "He's getting into the mechanical wagon!" he reported.

"Oh no!" Smurfette said. She knew that if they didn't hurry, they might not catch up with him.

Brainy was quickly calculating the probability. "Clearly, that distance is too great to—"

"Off ye go!" Gutsy interrupted, kicking Brainy off the fire escape with one swift boot. After all, they didn't have any time to waste!

"No! Gutsyyyyyyy!" Brainy screamed, passing floor after floor in midair. "Good-bye, blue world!"

Gutsy was the next to leap. "Come on, Smurfs!"

Their shouts echoed in the wind.

"Quickly!"

"Smurfabunga!"

"Use your hat as a chute, you ninny!"

It was hard to tell who was saying what, they were all falling so fast.

Except for the unmistakable voice of Grouchy. "Couldn't we just have taken the stairs?!"

Finally five white floppy parachute hats carrying the Smurfs fluttered gently down atop Patrick's cab. It was a perfect landing!

But Brainy was still mad about having been pushed. "Not funny, Gutsy!" he scolded.

"It was a little funny," Grouchy added his two cents in, chuckling.

"Shhh, Smurfs!" Papa put a finger to his lips. They all quieted down, as the taxi moved away from the curb and into traffic.

Like they had done on their first taxi ride, the Smurfs managed to blend in with the rooftop advertisement, helping them keep cover from anyone's prying eyes. Suddenly the cab skidded to a screeching halt. Inside the cab, Patrick's eyes shifted up toward the car's roof. Did he just hear something up there?

Chapter
12

"We're stopping. Hold on tight!" Papa warned as the taxi came to a stop in front of Anjelou Headquarters on Fifth Avenue.

Smurfette shoved Grouchy's hands away. "Not to me, Grouchy!"

Grouchy laughed. "Oh, did I do that? Sorry!"

Patrick barely had one foot out of the taxi before he heard the familiar sound of little blue creatures.

"Master Winslow! We really need your help," Papa called out to Patrick just as he was about to pay the driver.

Smurfette waved. "Yoo-hoo! Hey!"

Patrick raised his head to find the Smurfs standing on the roof of his cab.

"What are you doing here?" he cried out, astonished.

Gutsy was quick to reply. "What part of 'we need a Stargazer' don't ya understand, ya numptie!"

Patrick put a finger to his lips. "But you can't be out in public!" he whispered.

"Who are you talking to?" the cab driver shouted out the window at Patrick.

Patrick told him to hang on a second.

"If we could just have a quick look around in your predicting parlor," Papa inquired.

"We *really* want to go home," Smurfette said.

"Come on man, I gotta go!" the cab driver yelled again. He wanted his money. Now.

"Please, please," Smurfette begged.

When a few of Patrick's coworkers walked out of the Anjelou building, he panicked. "Okay, fine!" he said, throwing some cash at the cab driver and opening his jacket pocket for the Smurfs to jump inside. "Just come here."

Brainy wasn't too thrilled about the idea of getting into Patrick's jacket. "Whoa, hey!" he objected.

Patrick gave him a stern look before eyeing the others. "All of you," he commanded.

Knowing it was the only way into the building, Papa got in the coat. "Careful!" the older Smurf said.

Gutsy warned, "Watch the Smurfberries!"

Grouchy thought about the situation. "Oh no. No way am I going in there—," he complained.

"Be quiet," Patrick snapped at Grouchy.

One by one they leaped off the roof, with hardly a second to spare before the cab sped away. There was a moment of silence while everyone got as comfortable as possible inside Patrick's coat.

Brainy whimpered. "It's dark in here!"

"All right, who smurfed?" Grouchy choked and coughed.

With a final hushed "Shhh," Patrick double-checked

that everyone was hidden, and then quickly entered the building.

He tried to look casual as he approached the receptionist at the front desk.

Inside Patrick's jacket, Gutsy squirmed. "Get yer hand outta me kilt!"

"That's not my hand," Brainy defended himself.

Patrick tried to look like nothing was going on, but all that squirming around was making him want to laugh. "Hey, ticklish!" he muttered under his breath.

"Good morning, Mr. Winslow!" the receptionist greeted him. "Congratulations on your promotion."

Patrick slapped at the lump in his coat as he offered a quick "Thank you" and hurried toward his office. After checking that no one else was around, Patrick turned his attention to the Smurfs. "I hope you guys like desk drawers, because that's where you're gonna—"

"You're late," Odile barked, startling Patrick. She waved some papers at Patrick that he immediately recognized. They were his. From inside his desk!

"Ohhh-dile, ha-ha! You were in my office!" Patrick nervously stated the obvious.

"It's my building," Odile said brashly. "We have much work to do. The launch for Jouvenel is tomorrow night. Is your concept ready?"

"Ah, it's close." He began to explain, "I had a crazy morning—" Suddenly Patrick began to giggle as the Smurfs wiggled around inside his jacket.

Odile was not amused. "What are you doing?"

Patrick forced himself to speak calmly. "Um . . . nothing. It's just I'm excited. Excited! About all the concept ideas!"

Just then Gutsy growled. "Rrrrrrr."

"And hungry." Patrick pressed a fist into his coat. "Hungry for, uh, its success."

"Hmmm. Nervous energy." Odile considered it.

"Nervous energy's what's going on up in here!" Patrick nodded fiercely. He wrapped his jacket more tightly around himself.

"I like it. The fear of failure is a fabulous motivator." With a smug grin, Odile walked off toward the elevators.

"True that," Patrick muttered as he watched her go.

He hadn't even taken a step, when Odile's assistant appeared in the hallway. "Henri," Patrick greeted coolly, wishing he was finally alone already.

Henri stared Patrick square in the eye, and warned: "Make it work."

Patrick sighed. "You have no idea."

The moment Patrick got to his office he deposited the Smurfs onto his desk. As fast as he could, he closed the door and then attempted to block the windows.

"Why did I get the armpit?" Grouchy complained.

"Stop pushing me," Smurfette shoved Grouchy, hard.

"Are you guys *crazy*?" Patrick told them all to keep it down. "You're gonna get me fired!"

Smurfette tried to smooth her curls. "Ow, my hair."

Gutsy gasped for fresh air. "I couldn't breathe in there! It smelled like the business end of a sheep!"

Brainy was the first Smurf to take a long look around the office. "I don't see a Stargazer," he reported.

"I'm sorry, Master Winslow," Papa apologized on everyone's behalf. "But we badly needed to borrow your Stargazer—"

"I don't—have—a Stargazer!" Patrick cut in frantically. "Okay? It's not something people of this century just have. Especially here."

"Not happy," Grouchy said with a moan.

"Now, if you'll excuse me," Patrick continued, ignoring their disappointment, "I have to work." Then he plopped down at his desk and booted up his computer.

Then Papa had an idea! "Perhaps we'll sing to help you work faster. Then we'll go and get the Stargazer. Come along, Smurfs!"

Gathering around Patrick, the Smurfs began to serenade him. *"La, la, la-la-la-la, sing a happy song. La, la, la-la-la-la, Smurf the whole day long."*

Patrick tried to ignore them, but it was impossible.

"La, la, la-la-la-la, now you know the tune. La, la, la-la-la-la—"

Letting out an enormous, frustrated sigh, Patrick just couldn't take it any longer. "Okay, stop. Stop!"

They all trailed off and stared at Patrick in surprise.

"Oh c'mon. Nobody finds that song just the tiniest bit annoying?" Patrick asked.

"I find it annoying!" Grouchy said, raising his hand high in affirmation.

"Well, what do *you* sing at work?" Papa wanted to know.

"I don't sing at work," Patrick told them.

Smurfette gasped in horror. "What?!"

"*And* you have a wear a leash?" Gusty shook his head in pity.

"I know. How 'bout if we hum?" Smurfette suggested. Immediately the Smurfs began a low, muffled version of the La La song. As they hummed, the Smurfs began to explore Patrick's office. Patrick kept taking things away from them and putting them back where they belonged.

"Please stop humming," Patrick begged.

But they wouldn't stop. They kept on humming. And exploring. A coworker peered in through Patrick's office window. Desperately, he tried to block her view.

Work was becoming nearly impossible, and Patrick was getting a massive headache. "I need to hone my message here. Please," he pleaded with the Smurfs. "Be quiet."

"Ooohh. I've got a message," Brainy offered. "'Always chew with your mouth closed.' Papa taught us that!"

"That's good," Papa agreed. "You should use that, Master Winslow."

Smurfette added another one. "Or 'Dance and be happy!'"

"How 'boot 'Grab life by the grapes!'" Gutsy suggested.

There were tons more where those came from. Everyone kept throwing ideas at Patrick.

"I Smurf, therefore I am."

"Turn that frown upside down!"

"Hang in there!"

"Always bet on blue."

"Have a smurfy day!"

Excited to be useful, Smurfette tossed out her favorite Smurf saying. "I kissed a Smurf and I liked it!"

Papa turned to Patrick, proudly. "It's an embarrassment of riches. They're giving you gold."

Patrick rubbed his aching head. "There is no time and I need to do this on my own. Okay?"

Papa understood. "Yes. Very good. That's the honorable thing."

"Thank you," Patrick answered.

"But you should try to smurf a message that uplifts the whole village," Papa said, offering Patrick one last nugget of advice. "Right, Smurfs?"

Everyone nodded except Grouchy. He offered Patrick a sympathetic frown. "Welcome to my world."

Below Patrick's office, down on Fifth Avenue, Gargamel strode through some thick steam that rose from a manhole cover.

"I love emerging dramatically through the smoke," Gargamel said. He turned back to walk through it again. "It makes me feel so deliciously mysterious." He swung his cloak around like a supervillain's cape. "Also, it gives the skin a wonderful glow."

"Meow," reported Azrael, who was sitting on the sidewalk.

"What? Where, where?" Gargamel glanced around wildly.

"Meow," Azrael replied.

Finally Gargamel spotted it. On the building across the street was a window etched with a very familiar logo—the logo from the business card that had flown into Gargamel's hands when the Smurfs took off on the taxi. Gargamel pulled out the card and held it up to the building, trying to match the insignias.

"Curse! Oh, so close!" Gargamel said, assessing that the logo on the card was the exact opposite of the logo on the building.

"Meow," Azrael said once more.

Gargamel tilted his head over. "Oh. Theirs is upside-down. Idiots. They painted it wrong!" He looked again at the card, which he was actually holding upside down. The insignias matched after all. The building was the headquarters of Anjelou Cosmetics.

Azrael smacked himself in the head with a paw. How his master could be so dense, he'd never understand! Quickly he followed his master across the street.

The first floor of the Anjelou Cosmetics building held one of their huge customer stores. Gargamel and his cat wandered past shoppers getting makeovers and purchasing products. In the center of the store, Gargamel noticed a well-dressed woman, clearly in charge, addressing a group. He quietly approached.

Her assistant held out a jar of cream. The woman, Odile, took a small scoopful and dabbed a bit onto the face of a refined sixty-year-old lady.

"Be sure to demonstrate how this new anti-aging crème will make any woman look young, beautiful, and vibrant. It's almost magical," Odile told her sales staff.

Henri turned the jar so the Jouvenel label showed. "Astonishing, really," he praised with amazement.

Gargamel reached the front of the crowd. He leaned in to inspect the older woman's face. "I see no transformation," he spat. "Your potion has no power."

"Excuse me?" Odile said, arching her brow at this intruder.

"She's still an eye-offending dogfish if you ask me!" Grimacing, Gargamel turned his face away.

"Sir!" Henri exclaimed, appalled.

"This is my mother whom you are speaking of," an offended Odile cried out.

"I'm so sorry, I didn't realize." Gargamel took a longer look at the older woman and then at Odile. "How sad for you in thirty years."

Odile's face flushed red with anger. She turned to her assistant. "Henri, escort this lunatic out!"

Henri snapped his fingers, signaling a security guard.

"Lunatic?" Gargamel was insulted.

The officer wasn't coming fast enough. "Security!" Henri bellowed across the store.

"I am the great and powerful Gargamel," the wizard

introduced himself. "Lunatic?! Could a lunatic do this?"

Before the guard could reach him, Gargamel pulled a chopstick hair accessory out of a nearby woman's updo and poured a tiny drop of Smurf essence from inside his ring onto the tip of the stick. Then he placed the end of the stick on the old lady's face.

"Alaca-zootiful!" Gargamel incanted.

POOF!

Suddenly the woman's wrinkles disappeared. A youthful rosy color returned to her face. She looked at least twenty-five years younger.

The room was filled with gasps of awe.

Odile's eyes were wide with shock. *"¡Dios mio, Mamá!"* She turned to Gargamel. "How did you do that?"

"Yes, how?" Henri pleaded. "And seriously—me next."

Gargamel laughed them away. "So sorry but 'lunatics' and great wizards never reveal their secrets."

Odile's mother caught a glimpse of herself in a mirror. *"¡Dios mio!"* she exclaimed before passing out.

Turning on his heel, Gargamel called for his cat to follow him. "Come, Azrael. Now, where are my Smurfs?" he asked, as they headed for the shop exit.

"No, no, no. Don't go!" Odile rushed after Gargamel. "I must know. What did you just do?"

"Not telling," Gargamel said firmly.

Odile grabbed one of his arms. "Please, *señor*. Can you do that again?"

Gargamel glanced down at her arm, which was

wrapped tightly around his in an embrace. "You may attempt to persuade me," he said, finally.

"What is it you desire?" Odile whispered, leaning in to Gargamel, her voice raspy yet inviting. She gently touched his cheek. "Riches, fame, fortune? With my help, the whole world will know the name that is . . . uh . . . Garbagesmell!"

"Gargamel."

Odile corrected herself. "Yes, soon everyone will know the genius that is Gargamel."

Azrael meowed, trying to get Gargamel's attention. But Gargamel was too mesmerized by Odile's compliments to care what his cat was trying to tell him. Gargamel stomped on Azrael's tail, silencing him.

"I'm sorry, did you say 'genius'?" Gargamel asked.

Odile just patted Gargamel's arm gently in affirmation, a mischievous smile spreading across her face.

Chapter 13

When Grace arrived home, she heard singing from the fire escape.

"La, la, la-la-la-la."

Following the little voice, she discovered Clumsy outside, planting seeds in pots. "Hello! What are you doing?"

"Oh, just greening things up a bit," he replied.

Grace surveyed the things that Clumsy was planting: granola, bread, some pieces of corn, and a bean.

"That's very sweet," Grace began, "but I'm not so sure this stuff's gonna grow. Especially out here."

But Clumsy was very optimistic. He picked up a blue-colored berry, dropped it into a pot, and covered it with dirt. "We'll see. Smurfs have a very blue thumb."

"I can see that," Grace remarked, checking out his thumb. "So, where's everyone else?" she added.

"They went to get a Stargazer so Papa can smurf a Blue Moon to get us home."

"They went without you?" Grace asked.

"Yeah," Clumsy replied sadly. "I mean, who knows why," he added, leaning back on a pot and accidentally pushing it over the edge of the fire escape. It made a *thud* sound and then shattered.

"Phew," Clumsy said, relieved that no one was hurt.

"Hey! Watch it up there," shouted an angry voice from the sidewalk below.

The horrified look on Clumsy's face quickly turned to a smile as Grace burst out laughing. "Oops," she said softly. "Hey! Sorry!" she called down to the man.

She gave Clumsy a small grin. "Why don't we go inside?"

Grace got to work painting a jewelry chest, and Clumsy sat on top of it while he explained how the Smurfs ended up in New York.

"Then I tripped and fell off the cliff, and got sucked through the portal, so they all had to come get me. But, on the bright side, we did get to meet you and Patrick, so . . . I guess being clumsy *can* be a good thing."

Grace nodded. "Gosh, you know, I know how you feel. I'm so clumsy too."

"Nah!" Clumsy looked at her, surprised.

"I am, look at this! See this scar on my knee? I got this from a coffee table." Grace pointed to another white line on her elbow. "This one on my elbow, here? I got this jogging. Didn't see a mailbox."

Clumsy laughed. "So how'd you get to be named Grace and not Klutzy?"

Grace considered that. "Because I'm not *just* a klutz," she told him. "You know, I'm really good at other stuff too."

"Like what?" Clumsy was curious.

"I'm a pretty talented violinist. I'm a good painter. Oh, you know what? I'm a really good wife. Really good. You know, once I figured that out, I didn't trip so much anymore."

Clumsy wrinkled his nose, considering her words. "So, um—yeah, how long did it take to"—as he said it, he fell backward off the jewelry box and popped up to finish—"unfumble your feet?"

"Well," Grace answered, "about as long as it takes to realize you can be anything you want if you put your mind to it."

"Really?" Clumsy asked incredulously. The idea was one he'd never even been able to imagine before.

"Yeah, Clumsy. Nobody's just one thing. You could be anything you want to be!"

Clumsy was beginning to like the sound of that. Anything he wanted? That sounded incredible! He puffed out his chest confidently, and announced: "Hero Smurf!"

"Yeah?" Grace smiled encouragingly.

Clumsy thought about it some more. "Nah, probably not."

Grace was about to speak when her cell phone rang.

"Hi, Patrick," she said, hearing the joyful sound of la-la-la's in the background.

"Grace! Help! They're everywhere," he pleaded. "They won't stop singing. I cannot get a thing done. Please come get these guys."

In addition to the singing, Grace could hear the buzz of . . . what? A helicopter?

Suddenly she heard the boom of a crash—the sound of

Gutsy crashing the remote-controlled helicopter toy that Patrick had in his office.

In the background Grace caught Gutsy's smurfy voice saying, "Sorry 'boot that."

Quickly she hung up the phone and grabbed her purse, and she and Clumsy were on their way!

Across town, at one of New York's fanciest restaurants, Odile was treating Gargamel to lunch. Azrael was sitting in Henri's lap, licking caviar off a silver spoon, while Gargamel placed his order.

The instant the waiter left, Odile laid out her idea. "*Señor* Gargamel, I'll be frank. Every skin-care brand in the world would kill to get what you have in that ring."

Gargamel lowered his voice and came up with what he considered to be a very logical suggestion. "Not if we kill them first." At once he began planning. "Let's see, we'll need some knights, preferably in shining armor, some bowmen, and some poison arrows."

"I like the way you think," Odile replied with a wink.

"And some spikes to mount their heads on," Gargamel added.

"Well, it *is* all about presentation," Henri added, his tone snarky.

Just then the waiter came back carrying a huge tray laden with a variety of cooked meats. Gargamel snatched up a turkey leg and took a huge bite. Oily juice trickled down his chin.

Watching Gargamel devour the meal so mercilessly, Odile added, "Of course, all our testing will be animal-cruelty free."

Gargamel took another bite and answered, his mouth full of juicy meat. "What? I pay extra for animal cruelty, is that it?" But his thought was interrupted by a rude Azrael, who kept climbing up to try to steal some food off of Gargamel's plate. "Get out of here!" he snapped, shoving Azrael off the table.

Odile chuckled. "You have a wicked sense of humor. We like that, don't we, Henri?"

Azrael climbed back on the table. Gargamel knocked him down again. And again.

"The man is scintillating," Henri remarked, his statement overflowing with sarcasm.

"Yes, yes. Just assure me, *dahling*, that you can recreate whatever it was you did to my mother. But on a massive scale. Do that—and the world will worship you."

Gargamel bubbled with excitement. "Hear that, Azrael?"

"Meow."

"Worship. It rolls off the tongue like flesh from a . . ." Once again he couldn't find the right word to describe what he wanted to say. "Not *pilgrim* . . ."

"Martyr?" Henri provided.

"No."

"Heathen?" Henri tried again.

"No, no, no."

Gargamel turned to Azrael for help.

"Meow?"

"Heretic. Yes, thank you."

"Meow," Azrael replied with a slight nod.

"Now, to the matter at hand," Gargamel continued.

Odile wanted his potion so badly. "Sooo, we have a deal, *señor*?" She held out her hand for a shake.

With a sinister grin, Gargamel admitted there was still one piece of the puzzle missing. "Not quite, my sweet maiden. You see, first I must have my Smurfs!"

Odile and Henri exchanged frustrated glances.

All six Smurfs were back in a taxi, taking cover in a large Anjelou bag that Grace had gotten from Patrick's office. They were on their way back to the Winslows' apartment, and they were having quite a lot of trouble sitting still. Continuously they peeked out to take in the sights of their exciting new realm, but Grace pushed their heads down like playing a whack-a-mole game.

"You guys have to understand," she said, pushing Gutsy's head down for the hundredth time. "Patrick's under a lot of pressure, so if you could just lay low for a bit . . ."

The cab stopped at a red light.

Papa popped his head up. "You have my word of honor, Miss Grace. My Smurfs will not move from this bag."

"Okay." Grace breathed a relieved sigh.

Just then Gutsy poked up next to Papa. "Stargazer!" he cried out, noticing the thing they most needed in the window of a nearby shop across the street.

Instantly all the Smurfs were climbing up and jumping out of the bag.

"What?" Grace saw a poster in the window of giant toy store. The photo showed a man and a son looking through a telescope.

With Grace distracted by the poster, Gutsy managed to open the taxi door. "Stargazer! Let's go!"

"Everybody out!" Grouchy ordered.

Grace desperately tried to stop them. "No, no, no!"

"Let's go!" Smurfette announced, popping out of the cab before Grace could grab her.

Dodging cars, the Smurfs raced toward the store.

"Full smurf ahead!" Gutsy raised his hand like a conquering general in a war.

"Wait! Wait! Come back!" she yelled.

Grouchy shouted at a man in a car. "Hey! I'm walkin' here!"

Smurfette was awed by how quickly everyone in New York moved. "Can't everyone just slow down and enjoy life?!"

Papa saw danger approaching. "Wait for it . . . ," he warned. A skateboarder jumped in front of them. When the kid passed by, Papa gave the okay to keep on going.

"Gonna get me one of those," Gutsy said, watching the skateboarder jealously.

Grace, who had finally managed to get out of the cab, stared out onto the busy and dangerous Fifth Avenue traffic searching for the Smurfs. They couldn't just run wild through New York City! The city was a dangerous place for small blue creatures!

"Follow me, Smurfs!" Papa pointed at the toy store.

"Oh my gosh! Oh no!" Grace cried out, starting to follow them.

"Hey, lady!" the cab driver yelled, a reminder that Grace hadn't paid for the ride yet.

"Oh, right, right, right! Hold on!" She tossed a wad of cash over the seat and then crossed three lanes of traffic to where the Smurfs were.

Near the entrance to the store, Papa gave instructions. "When we get inside, spread out and find that Stargazer!"

A car sped by. Gutsy ducked. "Quickly, under the trolley."

A minute later, the Smurfs were safely across the street, at the store, and ready to do some serious shopping.

In the now-quiet office, Patrick's mind was blank, except for an occasional "La, la, la" wandering through. He had no ideas for the new campaign. But instead of focusing harder on his work, he found himself looking at one of the Web pages from the morning on his computer. He couldn't stop staring at one photograph: the Blue Moon.

Patrick was about to click out of the browser, when he had the seed of an idea. *Hmmm. The Blue Moon . . .*

He cut and pasted the photo from the Website into a clean new document. The moon wasn't really blue, until Patrick added color. Now, it was a true blue. Smurf blue.

Unwittingly, Patrick started humming the La La song out loud and scribbling down some text to go alongside the photograph.

BRRIING!

The loud ring startled Patrick, snapping him out of his deep thought. He looked at the number on the caller ID; it was Grace. But before she could say anything he blurted out, "Hey, I was just thinking about you."

"Patrick!" Grace shouted. "The Smurfs are AWOL!"

"Are you running?" Patrick held tight to the phone.

"I'm fine, but I need your help. I'm afraid they're going to get themselves killed." A car honked at Grace.

"Sweetie, they're fine," Patrick tried to calm his wife. "They can send us a tiny thank-you card when they get back to 'shroom town—right after they invent paper."

"Patrick, they need you."

"Honey . . . ," Patrick began.

At that moment Grace lost sight of the Smurfs. She began to panic even more. "Patrick, *I* need you. Oh my gosh," she cried. "Please hurry."

"All right. Where are you?"

Patrick hung up and was out the door in a flash.

Odile's town car pulled up in front of the Anjelou building, with Gargamel and Azrael in tow.

"No, it's not going to work," she yelled into her cell phone, stepping out of the car. "The man is a lunatic.

I don't know. He needs Smoops."

"Smurfs," Gargamel corrected her as he followed her into the building.

"Smarps," Odile repeated incorrectly into the receiver as she disappeared inside the building.

Gargamel said it, loud and forceful. "Smurfs. Smurfs! With an—urf!" He sighed in frustration.

As they were walking into the cosmetics building, Patrick, who was rushing out in a panic, ran smack into Gargamel. "Sorry," Patrick apologized immediately, but dashed off again in a hurry. "I'm so sorry," he echoed once more as he ran.

"You call that groveling, you fool?!" Gargamel called to him angrily.

But Patrick was already on his way down the street.

"Meow," remarked Azrael, who up until that point had been quietly perched in Henri's arms, basking in the special attention.

"Ah, every village has an idiot," Gargamel answered.

Azrael pointed his nose at Patrick. "Meow," he hissed fervently.

Gargamel surveyed the back of the running man. "What? You're right! That's him!" He shouted after Patrick. "Stop! Stop! Smurf-thief!"

"Meow!" Azrael bellowed, leaping out of Henri's arms to follow his master.

Chapter
14

The shelves of the toy store were stocked from top to bottom with the most incredible toys and games the Smurfs had ever seen.

"Stargazer, Stargazer, Stargazer," Smurfette chanted to herself as she worked her way through the crowded aisles.

She passed under a display of colorful stuffed zebras and elephants. Higher up, on the same shelves, she noticed a different fluffy animal that looked like a horse. Unlike a regular horse, this one had a golden horn on the top of its head. "So *that's* where all the unicorns went!" she whispered, amazed. "Why don't you run?" she asked the animals. "Have you forgotten how to be free?" Having never seen a toy store before, Smurfette didn't realize the stuffed animals weren't real!

Meanwhile, Papa and Brainy were searching for a precious Stargazer in another part of the store.

When they arrived at the bottom of the escalator, Brainy's eye widened in fear. They didn't have escalators in Smurf Village! "I'm not afraid to go off on my own," he said, trying his best to sound brave. "I just thought you might like the company."

"Fine, then, hang on," Papa assured him, grabbing hold of the handrail and jumping aboard.

Gutsy was also headed to the second floor, only he'd discovered another way to travel. "Ohhh, a Smurf cannon! Ah, the only way to fly." He climbed into a toy cannon and prepared himself for blastoff. "Perfect! Time to catch some air!"

BOOM! Gutsy went flying through the air, high above the second-story railing.

"SMURFABUNGA!" he screamed at the top of his little blue lungs.

Grace, who was nervously looking all over the store for any sign of the Smurfs, noticed the streak of blue propelling its way to the second level immediately. She started to run toward it.

With a smooth dive roll, Gutsy landed safely in an area filled with action figures and related toys. There, he began his search for a Stargazer.

Below him, still on the first floor, Grouchy was making his way up on a high ledge. "There's gotta be a Stargazer up here somewhere!"

Suddenly a nearby animatronic owl batted its wings.

"Aaaaahhhh! Predator!" Grouchy stumbled backward and fell, very nearly crashing to the floor. But instead, he landed on the paddle of a young girl playing paddleball with her friend. She swatted Grouchy, like a bouncy ball, straight into the candy department where he plopped down in a vat of blue candy.

"Aaaaaaah!" Grouchy popped up out of the vat as fast as he could, his mouth full of blue candy. "Ugh, Smurf droppings!" he cried, thinking they were gross. But then Grouchy realized that the blue bits were candy, full of chocolaty sweetness. "These are disgusting . . . ly tasty!" he declared, chewing happily.

Peering over the edge of the barrel, Grouchy spotted a doll, which he thought was real. Trying to be smooth, he sidled up next to her. "Well, hello there . . ."

Clumsy, who had spotted Papa and Brainy on the up escalator from afar, was desperately trying to reach them. "Ah . . . I'm coming, I'm coming!" he shouted, but no one heard his call. Unfortunately he was trying to climb up the down escalator, which he had jumped on by mistake, and was getting nowhere. "I'm coming, guys! Whoa."

On the up escalator Papa and Brainy were rapidly approaching the second floor. Brainy was in awe of the machinery. "What a fascinating device!" he exclaimed. "Pulleys and gears, and—"

THUD! THUD! In a flash Brainy tumbled off the handrail and Papa gently slid down to the floor.

Picking themselves up, they headed to the rear of the store.

"Papa, I'm telling you, we're never gonna find those—"

"Stargazers!" Papa exclaimed, spotting the telescopes up on a tall shelf.

Brainy calculated the distance from the floor to the Stargazers. "They're dangerously high!" he reported.

"You're right!" Papa nodded. "We're going to need something tall."

As Papa and Brainy plotted the Stargazer retrieval, Grace finally arrived on the second floor. She began to search for the Smurfs, failing to notice the giant teddy bear being wheeled in a cart by Papa and Brainy that was gliding along smoothly behind her, making its way toward the telescope display.

"Don't you think someone will notice us?" Brainy asked Papa.

Papa wasn't concerned. "Just act natural."

"Grrr . . . I'm a bear!" Brainy said.

Papa laughed. "Brainy!"

Unaware that Brainy and Papa had found the Stargazers, Grouchy was relaxing in the arms of his new friend. Little did he know she was just a doll, placed there to advertise the delicious candy he had inhaled earlier. He leaned back and took a long, fake sip from a candy soda bottle. "I'm just tired of the whole dating game. Just say who you are and be who you say."

The doll didn't reply. But she did smile. In fact, she was always smiling at Grouchy. He liked that.

Meanwhile, Clumsy was still stuck on the down escalator, trying to make his way up. "Still coming, guys! Oh, hold still, stairs!"

A little girl took notice of him and couldn't contain her excitement. "Whoa, look at the stair-climbing toy!" she remarked to her parents.

"Careful," they warned, as the girl reached to grab Clumsy.

The second he felt her cold fingers close tightly around his waist, Clumsy knew he was in trouble. He tried to stay as still as he could.

Suddenly another girl noticed the Smurf. "I want one too! Mommy!"

In another part of the store, Smurfette discovered an eerie display of disembodied doll heads. The bodyless heads frightened her. "Creepy," she said, her breath shaky. "I hope they weren't looking for a Stargazer too." She turned around and rushed away from there, repeating her earlier chant, "Stargazer, Stargazer, Stargazer," for luck.

Her fear faded as she came upon something wonderful—a room full of clothes, just Smurfette's size. "Dresses!" she exclaimed, overwhelmed with enthusiasm. "You mean I can have more than one kind of dress?! What!" She would have to take a short break from searching for the Stargazer to explore this grand discovery!

Over at the cash register, the little girl presented Clumsy to the salesclerk. The frazzled employee tried to scan Clumsy, hoping that a price would appear, while parents and kids gathered around the desk begging for similar toys.

Every time that laser zapped Clumsy on the forehead, his poor little eyes crossed. It was giving him a headache!

"I want one of those blue animatronic things!" one parent insisted.

"I'll take three!" another called out, waving a credit card.

"Do they come in pink?" someone else asked. "My daughter wants pink!"

The saleswoman couldn't figure out why the scanner wasn't working. "What aisle was this in?" she asked again.

"I'll take the floor model!" another voice called out from the back of the group.

"Not if I get it first!" someone shouted back.

Before long there was a riot at the checkout stand. "There's a line," an angry customer warned.

Everyone wanted to own a Clumsy Smurf!

Patrick, who had finally arrived outside the toy store, skirted past a gardener blowing leaves and rushed inside to look for Grace. He ignored the commotion at the checkout counter and began his search. Unfortunately, he had no idea that he had led Gargamel and Azrael right to the Smurfs.

"Smurf-thief! Stop!" Gargamel shouted, still outside. Then the wizard spotted steam billowing out of a subway grate, and turned around to walk dramatically through it. As he turned, Gargamel saw what Patrick had missed.

Propped up in the store's window display, Grouchy— who was on a serious sugar high by now—was lounging in the arms of his new girlfriend doll.

"Do I use my grouchiness as a wall because I'm afraid to be vulnerable?" he asked her. "You bet. But I've got feelings. The other day I was reading *Eat, Smurf, Love* and I—," he went on, without realizing that danger was lurking just outside the window.

Outside, Gargamel opened his ring, ready to use Smurfette's magical essence to capture Grouchy. But the ring was empty. "Oh, I can't be out already! What was I thinking, wasting my only drop of Smurf essence on that stupid hag?!"

"Meow," Azrael suggested.

Gargamel followed the cat's gaze and discovered the man with the leaf blower working outside. An idea began to take shape. . . .

With all the mayhem at the cashier counter, Clumsy managed to escape the gaggle of kids and parents who were shouting for him. "Keep your smurfs to yourself! Don't you people have any boundaries?" he shouted as he ran for cover, dashing right in front of Patrick's feet.

A crowd of kids and parents followed Clumsy, knocking Patrick to the floor in their rush to capture the blue toy.

Over in the doll aisle, Smurfette had also been spotted while trying on a bunch of dresses. Smurfette thought the kids were after the dresses, not her. "Hey! This dress is mine!" she cried out.

Luckily, Grace appeared and scooped Smurfette up in the nick of time. "Smurfette!" Grace called out, relieved, and tucked Smurfette into her purse and out of sight.

"Wait, I'm shopping!" Smurfette replied, popping her head up and pointing at all the clothing. She wanted to try on the rest! After all, she'd never been surrounded by so many different outfits in her life.

"Let's shop later," Grace said. It was time to escape.

Meanwhile, Patrick was searching the floor for Clumsy. He'd just seen him by the cash register. . . . Where could he have gone? "Clumsy?!" he shouted, looking around frantically.

"Patrick! Patrick, help!" Clumsy came out from behind a display.

"Clumsy, come here!" Patrick scooped him up and held the Smurf high, out of a little girl's reach.

"A giant's after me," Clumsy said, frightened. He pointed at the girl. "She's huge!"

"Hey, that's mine," the girl told Patrick.

"I'm sorry, little girl," Patrick told her. "But this one's not for sale."

The sweet-looking girl kicked Patrick in the shin.

"Oww!" Patrick shot back, hopping around in pain.

"MOMMY!" The girl screamed so loud, it echoed through the store.

Scared, not only for Clumsy, but for his own safely as well, Patrick quickly tucked Clumsy inside his jacket and hobbled away.

At the customer service counter, more and more people had gathered to demand little blue dolls.

Grouchy, safe for the moment, was still in the window, chatting with his green stuffed girlfriend. "Don't ever forget that for one magical moment, our two worlds met. And I wasn't grouchy. I wasn't." He stopped and looked at her. "Can you just say one thing?! Please! I'm dying here!"

That's when he heard the noise. Loud and scary and way too close.

VRRROOOM!

Gargamel had entered the toy store carrying the gardener's leaf blower on his back. The wizard held the blower tube high, and changed the setting from "blow" to "vacuum."

Directing the vacuum tube down, Gargamel approached the candy window.

THWOOP!

Grouchy was the first Smurf to be sucked into Gargamel's new Smurf–catching machine.

"That's one!" Gargamel cheered. He began to walk through the store, searching for the others.

Chapter
15

Papa and Brainy were still trying to get a Stargazer off the wall display. They were precariously perched high on the big bear's nose, but still they couldn't reach the telescope.

Brainy analyzed the situation. "Technically, when loading cargo on the head of a bear—"

Papa cut him off. "Brainy, just pull!"

As Brainy reached forward, teetering toward the Stargazer, something came swinging down from overhead, snatched the telescope, and landed safely on the bear's snout. It was Gutsy!

"Ahoy, mateys!" he greeted. "What are you waiting for? We're drawing a crowd!"

In an instant they were surrounded by a group of kids who had spotted Gutsy soaring through the air, and were now pursuing him.

"Show-off!" Brainy muttered.

Squinting at the children, Papa realized what was going on. "Oh dear! They think we're toys!"

"Hold on to your hats, boys, it's about to get grizzly," Gutsy said as the first kid rammed into the bear.

The bear shook wildly. "Hold on to his ears!" Brainy quickly suggested.

"Just hold on to that Stargazer!" Papa told Gutsy.

So many kids were shoving the bear that it began to tremble, then tip.

"Aaaaah!" Gutsy, Brainy, and Papa all screamed as the bear crashed down.

Displays fell like dominoes; toys, stuffed animals, and games splattered across the floor. The kids were scrambling over the cascade of toys, desperate to get to the Smurfs.

Using the bear as a springboard, the three Smurfs bounced. Gutsy quickly found a skateboard and pulled Brainy and Papa onto it. "C'mon, Smurfs."

"Go, go, go!" Papa chanted as they rolled out of the crowd of greedy kids.

Gutsy steered the skateboard. "I'll have you at rammin' speed in no time! Hold on!"

Brainy looked over his shoulder. "I think we lost them!"

"Duck!" Gutsy commanded as he navigated under a toy display.

Brainy didn't lower his head fast enough, and it smacked right into the shelving.

"Again with the head!" Brainy cried out, touching his new bump.

"Get in the way, and I'll caber-toss ya!" Gutsy warned whoever crossed their path.

"Where'd you learn how to drive?!" Brainy asked, his voice full of fear.

"You think you can do better?" Gutsy asked, turning to face his challenger.

"Yes, I do believe I can do better!" Brainy replied.

Papa warned them both. "Stop bickering!"

The stubborn Smurfs argued on and on, not paying attention to where they were headed. The skateboard continued to zoom forward—directly into danger. Gargamel had arrived on the second floor of the store and was eager to put his Smurf vacuum even further to the test.

THWOOP! THWOOP!

Brainy and Gutsy were immediately sucked up into the leaf blower.

"Two more!" Gargamel cackled cheerfully.

"Brainy! Gutsy!" Papa called out to them. He had managed to lose Gargamel for a moment by sliding under a shelf. But just for a moment.

"Papa," Gargamel growled, setting out to catch the most important Smurf of all.

At that very moment Grace stepped into the aisle and saw Gargamel standing there with his vacuum aimed to suck. Frightened by the sight, she turned to run. But Smurfette, who had poked her head out of Grace's purse, caught someone's attention.

"Grace!" Smurfette warned, but it was too late.

"Meeeooww!" Azrael howled, leaping onto Grace's shoulder and knocking the purse from her hand.

Smurfette tumbled out and seeing Azrael, began to run.

"No!" Grace shouted.

"You again! Get your paws off me," Smurfette snapped at the mean cat.

"Bad kitty!" Grace said, swatting the cat with the purse.

While Azrael was distracted, Smurfette ran for cover.

"I hate that cat!" Smurfette called out as she turned the corner and entered a new department loaded with shelf displays. She tried to find an escape route, but at the end of the aisle, Smurfette discovered Gargamel was already there, waiting for her.

"Come here you little—" He crooked a finger at her. "Ha!"

"Gargamel."

Smurfette glanced around and noticed that Papa was on his way to rescue her. She had to stall. . . .

"Ah, Smurfette, more lovely than ever," the wizard crooned.

"Oh Gargamel," Smurfette replied. "I guess you've outsmarted us again." She pretended to be afraid.

Grinning wildly, Gargamel aimed the vacuum hose at her. He revved up the engine and pointed the tube. . . .

Suddenly, Papa Smurf soared by on his skateboard. "Smurf's up!" Papa cried, pulling Smurfette onto the board.

"Or not," Smurfette teased as together they zipped down another aisle.

And yet, there was still a *THWOOP!*

Instead of Smurfette, Azrael, who had been right on Papa's heels, got sucked up by Gargamel! The vacuum motor strained as Azrael's wriggling tail stuck out from the tube.

"Azrael. Azrael, what are you doing?" Gargamel tugged the cat's tail.

"Meow!" Azrael's reply echoed from inside the vacuum.

"Out! Out!" Gargamel told the cat. "Get out of my suckamajig!" Gargamel smacked on the tube, trying to pop Azrael free.

Just then Patrick appeared. "Let me help you with that." He quickly flipped the switch on the leaf-vac, and the motor reversed.

Pressure built as the machine grew louder.

"Ah, thank you, kind sir," Gargamel said absentmindedly at first, until he took a good look at his helper. "You!?" As he realized who it was, the vacuum tube jolted to the side.

BOOM!

Azrael shot out as if from a cannon.

"Meeoooww," the cat cried as he slammed into a display of merchandise.

Gargamel was blown backward by the force of the leaf blower expelling the cat.

BOOM! BOOM! BOOM!

Three Smurfs also shot out of the vacuum.

"Aaaaaahhhhh!" Brainy shouted as he popped out.

"Yaaahooooo!" Gutsy enjoyed his second cannon ride of the day.

"Ow!" Grouchy moaned.

"Oof," the wizard grunted, as the force from the leaf blower hurtled him backward into the open elevator. The doors closed with a gentle ding.

Grace sidled up behind Patrick, who was standing in front of the elevator doors.

"Impressive," she remarked, complimenting his rescuing skills.

Patrick blushed. "Thanks."

"I'll get the Stargazer," Grace told him.

"I'll go get the Smurfs."

From underneath a pile of lunch boxes, Azrael meowed softly.

The elevator made its way to the first floor and by the time the doors reopened, the police had arrived. Still struggling with the blowing motor, Gargamel bumbled out of the elevator.

"That's him." The gardener pointed at Gargamel. "He took it right off my back. Leaf-blower thief!"

A cop lifted Gargamel to his feet and began to make the arrest. "Please stand up, sir."

The toy store staff and customers crowded around to watch.

"You're going downtown," a second officer said.

"Unhand me!" Gargamel tried to pull away.

"Do not resist," the second officer warned Gargamel as the first officer attempted to link Gargamel's wrists with handcuffs.

Kicking and scratching, Gargamel fought against being

arrested. "Unhand me, heathen, or suffer the wrath of the great and powerful—GLAAAAADGADIGGY."

The second cop ended Gargamel's rant by zapping the wizard with a taser, forcing him into a deep sleep. Gargamel flopped to the floor like a fish.

Later, after the Smurfs were all safely back in Patrick and Grace's apartment, Papa stood out on the fire escape using the telescope to chart stars and make calculations. All around Papa, Clumsy's plants had begun to sprout in their pots.

Brainy, Gutsy, Clumsy, and Grouchy waited patiently in the living room.

"Oh, dear, Papa should be done by now," Clumsy said, staring at their smurfy leader through the window.

Grouchy was tired. "Yeah, enough with the suspense. I want to go home."

Brainy agreed. "Me too."

Even Gutsy was done with the New York City adventure. "Now that that wily wizard's got our scent, it's a whole new wager. Without that Blue Moon, our giblets are gravy."

While the Smurfs waited for news from Papa, Patrick was busy working in his office.

"La, la, la-la-la-la," Patrick sang the catchy tune as he

© Peyo

opened a computer file on his laptop. He cut and pasted his retouched picture of a truly blue Blue Moon into a document. The image was beautiful.

His finger hovered over the 'send' button, but he couldn't get himself to hit it quite yet. Instead, he studied his advertisement. It was new. It was different. But was it what Odile *wanted*?

"The one that's inspired?" he asked himself. Patrick switched out the advertisement and pulled up another one he'd made. This ad was a much safer, simpler, and more traditional design. "Or the one that won't get me fired?"

He went with the less risky choice and attached the safer design to an e-mail. Then Patrick typed a message to Odile:

Odile, pending your approval, it's ready to go to the billboard agency.

Patrick sent the advertising copy. "Well, there goes nothing."

Leaning back in his office chair, he breathed out a deep, heavy sigh.

In the bedroom Grace was brushing Smurfette's hair with a doll-size comb. Doll dresses from the toy store were laid out on the bed.

"I don't understand. How can you be the *only* girl in the village?" Grace asked.

"Well, see, I wasn't brought by a stork like the others,"

Smurfette explained. "I was created by Gargamel to trap the other Smurfs."

Grace shook her head. "Wow. Then what happened?"

Smurfette looked up at Grace. "Papa saved me. He cast a special spell and then helped me become the Smurf I was meant to be."

"That is amazing."

Grace held out a mirror so Smurfette could see the back of her new hairdo. Smurfette was thrilled! She couldn't wait to pick out a new dress and show off to everyone.

Chapter 16

"Well, it's off," Patrick announced, walking into the living room and setting his laptop down on the coffee table. "Time to either celebrate or file for unemployment."

When the Smurfs didn't respond, Patrick took a closer look at their faces. "What's wrong? You guys look like death smurfed over."

"I'm sure we'll be fine," Brainy said, nervously.

"That one's hypersmurfalatin'," Gutsy announced, blowing Brainy's cover.

"Tell me about it," Grouchy added.

"All this waiting's killin' us!" Gutsy admitted.

"Yeah," Clumsy agreed.

"I know the feeling," Patrick replied. "Better yet—I know the cure!" he added, going into a cabinet and pulling out his video game set. Patrick set up a video game on the TV that simulated being part of a band. He showed the Smurfs how to play, and then he cranked up the music. The Smurfs gathered round with excitement.

"Whoa!" Gutsy exclaimed in amazement. He'd never seen anything like it before!

"You just match the colors with the buttons," Brainy pointed out.

"Wow!" Grouchy blurted out, actually happy for once.

Patrick started rockin' out to one of his favorites, Aerosmith's "Walk This Way" on his guitar, to show them how it was done. Clumsy, who was starting to get into the groove, tripped over his feet and fell right on top of the drum kit. Discovering the drumsticks, Clumsy picked them up and started pounding away to the beat. It was the perfect instrument for him—banging around and making noise was his specialty!

Patrick took a break and offered the guitar to Grouchy. "You try it."

Grouchy began playing the notes like a pro. The points were racking up on the screen. The other Smurfs cheered him along.

"Hey, go, Grouchy!"

"Nice one!"

Even Grouchy was having a great time. "Hey, look at me, guys, I'm shredding!"

Then Patrick began to sing and invited the Smurfs to join in. They all belted together. He looked at the Smurfs, who were dancing all over the living room, like real rock stars, and decided to show them a little rock star move. He stuck his tongue out as far as it would go and began swirling it around, the way hardcore rock singers sometimes do. "Rock face," he explained, but the Smurfs weren't listening— they were already busy making crazy rock faces.

Grouchy stepped up and began rapping to the beat. He made up words as he went along.

Even Elway joined the fun, stepping on the kick drum pedal to add to the beat.

But it was Clumsy who was the star of the show. "Check out Clumsy!" Gutsy called out.

Clumsy twirled the drumsticks between his fingers like he'd been drumming his whole life. When he tossed a stick into the air, everyone ducked, but Clumsy easily caught it. They were all amazed.

"Oh Clumsy," Patrick cheered. "You've found your niche!"

"Clumsy, holding it down!" Grouchy praised.

"Look at him go!" Gutsy cried.

Another solo was coming. "Come on, Gutsy!" Patrick encouraged.

Up to the challenge, Gutsy jumped onto the guitar to perform a *Riverdance* routine. Lights were flashing as the points kept on coming. Gutsy nailed them all.

"Yeah, Gutsy!" Grouchy yelled, dancing a bit himself. "Get down wich yo bad Smurf!"

"Go, Gutsy!" Brainy egged him on.

"Yeah, that's right!" Grouchy watched the lights being captured.

Gutsy did a flip on the neck of the guitar. "Whoa!" He surprised himself!

"Get your Smurf on!" Grouchy said.

"Gutsy!" Brainy cheered.

"Nice!" Patrick added.

With a final flourish, Gutsy took a huge leap and landed on the coffee table. "That was rare!" Gutsy exclaimed.

The Smurfs added a few la-la-la's to the rhythm of the song. Clumsy kept on drumming in perfect time.

"La, la, la-la-la-la, la, la, la-la-la."

When the song ended, the stress of the day was completely forgotten.

The music was still ringing in everyone's ears when Grace and Smurfette came into the living room.

"Hey, guys, how do you like my new dress?" she asked.

Grouchy, Gutsy, and Brainy just stood there, awestruck.

"Sorry, boys," Smurfette said, realizing they had been in the middle of something. "Don't let little ol' me interrupt."

Just then the air conditioning vent she was standing on began to blow air up her dress, swooshing it this way and that. "Whoa, is there a draft in here?!" Smurfette said, quickly grabbing hold of the edges of her skirt and trying to hold them down. "Oh. Okay, that's not what I had in mind."

"Ahhh," was all the now light-headed Brainy could muster up.

"Are ya thinkin' what I'm thinkin'?" Gutsy whispered to Grouchy.

Gutsy rushed over to stand on the air vent alongside her. "Oh, yeah, that cools the giblets. Nothing like a cool breeze."

"I think I just smurfed in my mouth," Grouchy groaned, grossed out by Gutsy.

Grace began to giggle so hard she could barely stop.

Just then a beeping noise made Patrick glance over at his computer screen. His e-mail account was buzzing. He dashed over to see what Odile said. "Aha!! It's approved! She approved it. She approved the ad!!" Patrick was jumping up and down.

"She loved it?!" Grace said, joining him in a happy dance.

"Well," Patrick started, "it said 'approved.' Coming from her, that's love."

"Oh my goodness." Grace hugged him.

"Go, Patrick!" the Smurfs whooped in joy.

Clumsy climbed up on the table to celebrate with the others when he tripped and fell onto the laptop keyboard. No one noticed when Clumsy's klutzy feet brought up the image of the Blue Moon ad—the one Patrick had decided *not* to send to Odile. As Clumsy struggled to stand up, his unsteady heel clicked across the keyboard, hitting a flurry of keys in the process. Unbeknownst to anyone, his clicking managed to detach the approved ad from the e-mail and attach the Blue Moon ad instead.

Patrick turned to the computer and readdressed the e-mail to the ad agency, preparing to forward them the approved ad without realizing it had been accidentally switched.

"Do it!" Grace encouraged him.

"I will do it!" Patrick said gladly.

"Go, go, go!" Grace chanted as Patrick drafted an e-mail.

"Tomorrow this will be on every billboard in New York City!" Patrick hit a single key on the keyboard. The e-mail was sent.

"It's a go!" Gutsy said with a whoop.

Just as the e-mail sped away into cyberspace, Papa came in off the fire escape.

"Well done, Master Winslow," he said.

The Smurfs all turned around to look at Papa.

"Oh! Hey, guys, Papa's back!" Smurfette announced, overjoyed.

But Papa looked weary; he was not in the mood to celebrate.

"Papa, are your calculations done?" Brainy asked.

"Yeah, are we going home?" Grouchy added.

"Yeah, we're nearly out of Smurfberries," Gutsy warned.

Papa sighed. "It's proving more difficult than I'd hoped."

The other Smurfs all gasped. "But, we're going home. Right?" Clumsy asked, hopefully.

"Of course, just not tonight." Papa went to get his canvas sack. "Now, everyone needs their Smurfberries, and then it's off to bed. We'll have a lot to do tomorrow, and you'll need your strength."

Like any caring parent, Papa set about tucking his little Smurfs in for the night. The Smurfs had each nestled into different comfy corners. Smurfette was curled up in a hat, Brainy was covered with a washcloth, and Grouchy was using an oven mitt for a sleeping bag. Gutsy, always the risk-taker, had made a comfy spot for himself in Elway's fur.

Papa made his way to each of his Smurfs, making sure they were cozy and that they'd eaten their Smurfberries. Little did he know that Patrick was watching from the shadows.

"Ah, I was hoping I'd be sleeping in my mushroom tonight," Brainy said, tucking his hands behind his head as if they were a pillow.

"I miss the other Smurfs," Smurfette admitted.

"Me too," Clumsy said. "I've never slept the night away from home before."

"Well, there was last night," Grouchy reminded him. "But who could sleep?"

"Shh. Hush, hush now, Smurfs," Papa Smurf told them. "Everything is going to be just fine."

"Papa?" Smurfette asked. "Do you really believe that we are ever going to get home to the other Smurfs?"

The eldest Smurf tried his best to sound reassuring. "Don't worry, we'll be reunited with the other Smurfs soon enough."

From where he stood, Patrick could hear Papa mutter softly to himself, "If only the stars will align."

Patrick snuck away, wishing there was something more he could do to help.

"I miss the other Smurfs," Brainy repeated. "Chef Smurf, Hefty Smurf, Jokey Smurf . . ."

The other Smurfs added to the list.

"Greedy, Narrator . . ."

"Painter, Baker . . ."

"Harmony."

"Oh, I miss Complimentary Smurf," Brainy said. "Always has such nice things to say."

Smurfette laughed. "I'll tell you who I don't miss," she added. "Passive-Aggressive Smurf."

"Yeah," Clumsy agreed. "Always so nice but when he leaves, you feel bad."

The Smurfs all smiled to themselves, awash in memories, as they coasted off to sleep.

In downtown New York City, a furious Gargamel was locked in a cold, dark jail cell.

A moth fluttered by the scratched cell window. "Oh, hello little moth," Gargamel whispered to the creature. "Perhaps with your help, I'll find a way to get them back." He yearned for revenge on both Patrick and the Smurfs.

The moth fluttered through the steel bars and settled softly in Gargamel's palm.

"Oh, you and I are kindred spirits, little one—both of us meant to soar. Go back and bring a glorious army of eagles to free me. Now fly, tiny eagle. Fly and bring your brethren. Fly . . . fly . . . fly."

At Gargamel's command, the moth flew away.

When the Smurfs were finally fast asleep, Papa returned to the fire escape to continue searching for the Blue Moon through the Stargazer. But he was becoming increasingly uncertain that it would appear again.

Patrick decided the old man could use a treat. He went out onto the fire escape holding two mugs full of steaming liquid, one of which had a little bendy straw sticking out of it. He offered that mug to Papa.

"Hey. I'm guessing you've got a long night ahead of you. You guys drink coffee?" Patrick asked.

Papa chuckled. "Is a Smurf's butt blue?" he joked, reaching for the cup. While Papa drew symbols on a piece of paper, Patrick chatted. "So, that weird guy in a ratty bathrobe at the toy store"—he paused—"he's not *really* a wizard, is he?"

Papa pinched his lips together. "Gargamel? He's not the smartest of the sorcerers. But dangerous just the same." After a sip of coffee Papa went on. "Back home I could hold him at bay with a spell or two. But here, without my books and potions, well, today we got lucky. But next time, who knows."

"So what are you going to do?"

"I'll do anything and everything I can do to get my Smurfs home," Papa replied. "I won't ever give up. They're my family, and you never give up on family."

Patrick nodded, clearly impressed. "Doesn't it freak you out sometimes having all those little guys depending on you? What if you mess up? How'd you know when you were ready?"

Papa set down his work. "Here," he said, patting his knee. "Come, sit on Papa's lap."

"Probably not the best idea," Patrick said, wondering how that would be physically possible without crushing Papa to death.

"You're right, scratch that." Papa smiled. "Let me ask you something," he continued. "Why did you come for us today when your Grace called?"

"Because she needed me," Patrick said without hesitation. "I could hear it in her voice."

"Uh-huh. That's what being a Papa is. When the time comes—you just do. And knowing what to do doesn't come from up here." Papa pointed to his head. "It comes from here where it matters most." Papa pointed to Patrick's belly area.

"My spleen?" Patrick asked, confused.

Papa laughed. "No. Your heart! I'm trying to have a moment here, you whippersnapper."

It was quiet while they both drank sips of their coffee and stared up at the stars.

"You're a good papa, Papa," Patrick said at last.

"You'll be a good one too," Papa assured him.

As the sun began to rise on the jail yard, Gargamel was sitting on a bench, waiting for his rescuers. A huge, menacing man named Bubba and his silent friend were lifting weights in a corner.

"What you doing, man? Come on, get that weight up," Bubba coached.

After a few more lifts, Bubba set aside the barbell and the two men approached Gargamel.

"You know what happens to people who sit on my bench?" Bubba threatened the wizard.

But Gargamel was not afraid. "Be gone, behemoth. For I've summoned forth a gaggle of noble eagles to free me from this confine."

"Get up, Grandpa!" Bubba barked.

Before Bubba could force Gargamel off the bench, a gray shadow crossed the jail yard from above. They looked up to see a flock of what appeared to be birds approaching.

Gargamel rose to his feet. "Ha-ha! You see? You see?! A dungeon isn't built that can hold the likes of Gargamel! Behold, my glorious army of—"

But it wasn't a flock of birds. It was a swarm of flies. And in a flash, Gargamel was covered by them. The moth from the night before fluttered proudly in the lead.

"Flies? Flies?!" Gargamel cursed the moth. "I said, 'Fly! Fly,' not 'flies,' you light-loving bug brain!"

The buzzing swarm lifted Gargamel off the ground, carrying him up and away from the jail yard.

"All right!" Gargamel had to keep his mouth partly closed to not swallow any flies. "Up, up, up! Up, you inglorious devils." He waved to the ground below. "So long, *les misérables!*"

"*Ouch!*" The flies had carried Gargamel smack into the plastic backboard of the basketball hoop. "Well, don't fly into it again—" At that, they smashed him into it, over and over again, as if trying to get out of a closed window.

"Go around it!" Gargamel instructed. "Arou—
GGARGLEELE! STUPID FLIES!"

"Wait! Take me with you," Bubba cried from below as
the flies finally managed to go around the backboard and
up into the sky.

Gargamel thought he was finally in the clear, until the
flies flew too close to the top of the jail's barbed wire fence.

"Are you *kidding* me?" Gargamel asked furiously, as his
orange jumpsuit snagged on metal spike after metal spike.

It took some effort, but the wizard shook himself free.

"To the castle for more essence!" he commanded.

It would undoubtedly be a difficult journey, but it was
his only escape. Soon he would be back in his castle in
Central Park, plotting once again his capture of the Smurfs.

Chapter 17

The next morning the Smurfs were busily tiptoeing around the apartment. Suddenly there was a creak in the hallway. "Shhh. Here they come. Here they come!"

Patrick and Grace slowly made their way into the living room. To their utter amazement, the Smurfs had surprised them by sprucing up their apartment! The seeds that Clumsy had planted earlier on the fire escape had already grown into lush, flowering plants. The vines snaked in through an open window and covered the walls, making their living room look like a blooming rainforest.

"Whoa" was all Patrick could say. Grace was also amazed.

"Pretty smurfy, if I do say so myself," Brainy gushed.

Then the Smurfs signaled for Elway, who trotted in carrying flowers for a tabletop arrangement in his mouth.

"That's a good boy," Gutsy told the dog. When Elway set down the flowers, Gutsy arranged them on the table. "There we go."

"Clumsy, did you grow all of this?" Grace asked.

He held out both hands. "Blue thumbs!"

"This is unbelievable!" Grace exclaimed. The smile on her face was bright as the sun.

Grouchy, who was still focusing on the flower arrangement, complained that the colors weren't evenly balanced. "I think there's too much pink."

"Just because your name is 'Grouchy' doesn't mean you always have to *be* grouchy," Clumsy responded.

Grouchy snorted. "Yeah, it does."

Grace went over to Smurfette and held up her hand. "Smurfette! High five!" The little Smurf held up her palm. Grace counted Smurf fingers and changed her chant to "High four!"

"High four," Smurfette echoed, and they slapped palms.

Just then Papa climbed in through the window, waving pages of notes excitedly.

"Great news! The stars have revealed the perfect time to smurf the Blue Moon!"

The Smurfs' cheers rocked the apartment.

"Smurftastic!" Brainy exclaimed.

"I never doubted it for a second," Grouchy said.

"It has to be done tonight between first star and high moon," Papa warned. "That's our only chance. But, we'll need a magic spell that works in *this* realm to open the portal home."

Papa turned to Patrick. "Master Winslow, a question, please."

"Yep, yep, shoot." Patrick waited to hear.

"Is there a place that sells spells?"

That was an easy one. "No."

Papa tried again. "Is there a place that proffers potions?"

Patrick didn't even think about it. "Yeah, no."

Papa wasn't giving up. "How about old books?"

Patrick nearly said "no" again, but then realized he *did* know one of those places. "Um . . . Wait, there's an antique book shop right near where I work." He struggled to recall the name. "Doctor—"

Grace remembered. "Doctor Wong's."

"Doctor Wong's . . . something." Patrick knew there was more to the title but he couldn't remember what.

It didn't matter, what he did remember was good enough for Papa. "Perfect! That will do!"

Smurfette jumped for joy. "Hear that, boys? We're almost home!"

"I LOVE being almost home!" Grouchy shouted, sounding the happiest he'd ever been.

"Yay!" Gutsy called out. "Smurf hug!"

"Smurf hug," Smurfette said warmly. And they all gathered round, holding one another in a big blue clump.

Papa invited Patrick to join the hug-fest. "Bring it in, big fella."

"Come on, Patrick, don't be shy!" Smurfette urged Patrick.

Grouchy shrugged. "If I can do it, you can do it."

Patrick leaned down and the Smurfs swarmed him.

"Smurf hug!" Clumsy cried out happily.

Grace smiled as Patrick tickled the Smurfs, laughing and playing, like he might some day with his own kids. It sent warm shivers up her spine. Patrick was going to make a great father, she just knew it.

Just then Smurfette looked out the window and noticed a beautiful sight. "Look! We don't have to make a Blue Moon. We've already got one."

"Really?" Grouchy asked, joining her at the window.

"Look, guys," Smurfette told them. "Right over there!"

Just beyond the Winslows' apartment, a new billboard ad was being installed. The Anjelou logo sparkled at the bottom of the photograph.

Patrick gasped, knocking Smurfs off him as he leaped up from the floor. "No. It isn't!"

"Hey. Smurfette's right. Look at the Blue Moon!" Brainy said.

"That's the Anjelou ad," Patrick informed them. Then he ran to his office.

When Patrick threw open the door, he was shocked to find that the space had been completely transformed into a nursery.

"What the—? What happened to my office?" he snapped.

Unfortunately, he was not as excited as the Smurfs hoped he'd be.

"We fixed it," Smurfette told him proudly, showing off the crib and changing table. "For the baby." She grabbed Clumsy around the waist. "Another Smurf hug."

The Smurfs all joined for another embrace, but Patrick moved past them. Luckily they hadn't moved his computer from his desk.

Fingers flying, Patrick frantically searched his outgoing e-mails. "No. No, no, no. This isn't happening. This isn't happening!" Anger rose in his face as he saw that the Blue Moon document was attached to his e-mail. Furious, Patrick turned to the Smurfs. "Someone sent this to the ad agency last night. Who messed with my computer?!"

Clumsy, remembering his run-in with Patrick's laptop the other evening, raised his hand timidly. "I . . . I, uh . . . I might have . . . sorta . . . tripped."

Patrick snapped at Clumsy. "Yeah? Well, you might've sorta gotten me fired. You sent the wrong file."

"Patrick." Grace cut in, trying to ease the tension. "It was just a—"

"What am I supposed to do, Grace?" Patrick yelled, his voice growing louder and angrier by the second. "You said they'd bring good luck. This is anything but good. I never should have let this happen. I should have said 'no.' I never wanted a house full of little people running around!"

This hit Grace hard and left her wondering if he wasn't *just* referring to the Smurfs. From the look on her face, it was clear she was deeply hurt.

Patrick realized what he'd said. "Blue! Little *blue* people," he corrected before rushing into the bedroom to get dressed for work.

Grace followed him. "Okay. Whoa. Patrick. What are you doing?"

"I'm going to try to save my job." Patrick threw on his shoes.

The Smurfs gathered in the bedroom doorway.

"We never intended to be a burden, Master Winslow," Papa Smurf told him.

"I'm smurfily sorry about what I—," Clumsy started.

"Stop saying 'smurf' for everything! What does that mean, anyway? Smurf?! Smurfity-smurf, smurf, smurf!" Patrick's anger was overflowing.

"Well, there's no cause for that kind of language, laddie," Gutsy told Patrick.

Glaring at Gutsy and the other Smurfs, Patrick stormed out of the apartment.

"Patrick, wait," Grace said, following him down to the curb. "Will you—Patrick, will you just stop and listen to me for a second. Please!?"

Patrick had never heard this tone in her voice before. "What?"

"Look, I'm really sorry about your job. Okay? And I hope you can straighten that out. But you are so not seeing the big picture." She stared deep into Patrick's eyes. "I mean, look around. Look what's happening right now! Of all the people on the planet, those magical little creatures chose us. Don't you see how absolutely amazing that is? It's a once-in-a-lifetime thing, Patrick. This is *our* Blue Moon. And if you don't stop for just a second and see that, you're going to miss it."

Having said what she wanted him to hear, Grace went back into the apartment.

But Patrick didn't even watch her go. He hailed a taxicab and went to work.

Chapter 18

Back inside Belvedere Castle, Gargamel angrily kicked his Smurf-essence-making equipment. "C'mon, come on, blast you!" He turned over every vial, peered into every tube. "There's gotta be some essence in here somewhere!"

"Meow," said his cat.

"Not now!" Gargamel barked, brushing Azrael aside.

"Meow," Azrael repeated.

"What? What?!" Annoyed, Gargamel stared at his cat. Azrael was looking at a still-glowing tube.

"Very, very, well done, my little friend," Gargamel complimented.

Azrael beamed proudly as Gargamel put the last tiny bit of the serum he'd made from Smurfette's hair into his ring.

"And to think I almost ate you that time."

"Meow!" Azrael was shocked.

"Come, Azrael." Gargamel swept his cloak around himself, ready to leave. "We must find this 'Patrick,' the rogue merchant. He will lead us to our elusive little blue quarry."

As he walked toward the Anjelou building, Patrick called the billboard company. "Don't you just have a switch or something to shut 'em off? *Tomorrow?* Are you kidding? Ron, Ron, if those ads don't come down now, I won't have a job tomorrow."

There was nothing the company could do. For today at least, the ads were up. And they were staying up.

Patrick couldn't go three steps without seeing a newly installed Blue Moon advertising poster. They were everywhere. Unable to bear it any longer, he sank down onto a bus stop bench and dropped his head into his hands.

All of a sudden, his cell phone chirped. Reluctantly, Patrick pulled it out of his pocket and read the text.

Call me so I can fire you, Odile

Patrick leaned back on the bench and sighed. "Smurf me." He'd call later.

When he reached into his pocket to put away the phone, Patrick found a card tucked inside. It was from Grace. The front read: *Baby's 1st Picture.*

Opening it, he found a photograph from the ultrasound of their baby, which he had missed. The appointment was yesterday, but with the Smurfs and all, he'd forgotten to ask Grace about it. He was so ashamed.

Patrick put a finger on the photograph, pretending to hold the baby's tiny hand in his.

Just then a child's squeal caused Patrick to look up. A young couple was helping their toddler take his first steps.

Patrick couldn't help but grin as the proud daddy scooped the baby up and twirled him around in delight.

Patrick looked back at the ultrasound picture. Then at the Blue Moon poster.

Suddenly, Patrick knew exactly what he needed to do.

Meanwhile the Smurfs had left Clumsy and Grace at the apartment to go out in search of the antique bookstore Patrick had told them about. They were standing at the subway entrance, hidden in the shadows while they discussed their plan.

Brainy looked around. "Where do you suppose this magic bookstore could be?"

Grouchy studied the subway train map. "We should take the F train to Lafayette Station. We'll be a couple of blocks away from the old bookstore."

Smurfette studied all the people coming in and out of the subway tunnel. "Um, aren't we worried we'll stand out?"

Papa took a closer look at the people. There was a street performer dressed like a silver statue. Another man dancing to his own beat wearing a tin on his head. Someone else in a frog costume was riding a unicycle.

"I don't think it's going to be a problem," Papa reassured them all.

The Smurfs hurried down to the platform, where the doors to the F train were closing.

"There it is." Papa pointed.

"Come on!" Gutsy said.

Smurfette was ready to get aboard. "This way!"

"All together now!" Papa got them to leap, just as the doors were shutting.

Papa made it in. The rest, well, they got stuck, smashed between the automatic doors.

"Aaaaagh!" It was a group yell.

"Oh smurf!" Papa helped them each to wiggle into the car.

Once they were all safely inside, the Smurfs realized that the subway train was like another world. Commuters were playing with small computers, reading books, and listening to music. No one was talking to anybody else.

Papa, Grouchy, and Smurfette found seats together. Gutsy and Brainy had taken shelter underneath the chairs. Everyone was so self-absorbed; no one seemed to notice the small blue creatures.

Gutsy wanted to explore. "Come on, Brainy. Let's look around this metal contraption."

Brainy was reluctant. "Are you sure about this?"

"Where's your curiosity?" Gutsy asked, climbing out from under the seats.

So Brainy followed him into the central aisle. Suddenly the train lurched and the two Smurfs were thrown backward into a man's briefcase.

"Look out!" Gutsy said, as another lurch threw them forward into a second briefcase. The first case hit them from behind, squishing them like a dazed Smurf sandwich.

Meanwhile, Papa struck up a conversation with the man

next to him. "Thank smurf it's Friday, huh? What a week!"

"Amen, brother," the man agreed.

"Well, we sing when we have a rough week!" Smurfette said. "Come on, guys."

"La, la, la-la-la-la, sing a happy song. La, la, la-la-la-la, Smurf the whole day long!"

By the time the train reached the next station, everyone on board had joined in the song.

"La, la, la-la-la-la, sing a happy song. La, la, la-la-la-la, Smurf the whole day long!"

"Everyone's so nice here!" Smurfette remarked as they got off the train.

That was until a businesswoman spotted the Smurfs. "Ah!! Blue rats!" she shrieked.

"Let's go!" Gutsy said.

The woman was trying to stomp on them with her high-heeled shoes.

The Smurfs scattered into the street and found cover under five empty popcorn bags. Poking out holes for their eyes, they bounced along the pavement, easily blending in with the other trash and litter.

"I hope we find this place soon, I can't see outta this—ah!" Grouchy bumped into a street pole. "Oh, for Smurfs' sake."

Gutsy laughed. "I thought that was why we left Clumsy behind!"

Grouchy snarled at him.

"It smells like butter," Smurfette complained.

"Where do you suppose this magic bookstore could be?"

Brainy asked, struggling to look around through the eyeholes.

Smurfette found it first. "There it is!" She quickly added with a shiver, "It looks creepy."

"It looks closed," Brainy announced.

Grouchy sighed. "Of course it's closed."

"We have to find a way in." Papa led the way. "Come on, let's get across this street."

BEEP! BEEP! A speeding car zoomed by, barely missing them.

At the shop's front door, the Smurfs removed the popcorn bags and slid through the narrow mail slot.

"Oh! My hip," Papa complained. "I'm getting too old for this," he added, rubbing his leg as the other Smurfs gently pushed him through the slot.

One after the other they went through, landing on top of one another, in a big blue pile.

"All right, everybody?" Gutsy asked, helping everyone up.

After allowing their eyes to adjust to the dark, the Smurfs looked around at the packed store.

"Wow," Smurfette said, overwhelmed by it all. The store looked run-down, but was stacked to the brim with books, skulls, wands, and potions lining the dusty shelves.

"This place looks creepy to me." Brainy agreed with Smurfette's first impression.

"It's not creepy," Gutsy replied. "It's different. I like it."

It didn't matter to Grouchy whether it was creepy or not. He just wanted to hurry. "Let's just get the book and get outta here."

But there was so much stuff everywhere.

"Where should we start?" Smurfette asked.

"We'll search every shelf," Papa ordered, undaunted. "This book of spells is our ticket home."

As the Smurfs searched the antique bookstore from top to bottom, Gargamel was on a hunt of his own—a Smurf hunt—on the streets of New York City. "I am but a simple wizard with a simple desire: limitless power and world recognition! Now, why does that have to be so hard?"

Azrael, who'd been walking with Gargamel, stepped out of the way to let the homeless person they'd met the previous day wander by. The man was absentmindedly singing. *"La, la, la-la-la-la."*

"Pardon me, please, wise sir," Gargamel exclaimed, stopping the man. "Please, please, where did you learn that ear-damaging squall?"

"It's your little blue men," the homeless person replied. "They went into the bookstore around the corner." He showed Gargamel the way. *"La, la la-la-la-la.* You know, that song is really annoying," the man said.

Gargamel agreed. Then he took off. "Cautiously ex-ciii-ted!" he cried, as he ran to the store. This was *the* moment—they were finally within his reach!

He would not fail again.

Grouchy tossed books off the shelves after he checked each title. "That's not it, that's not it, that's not it . . . hey! No, that's not it."

Brainy would have liked to take the entire library home. "Look at all these amazing books!" He stayed focused. "It's got to be in here somewhere," he said, checking another one. "No, this isn't it."

"Look out below!" Smurfette slid down the banister from the second floor. "Nothing up here, guys." She landed gracefully.

"I've got something, lads!" High on a shelf, Gutsy tugged at a heavy leather-bound book. Out it came, crashing to the ground in a plume of dust.

Recognizing the book's cover, Papa was thrilled. "Great job, Gutsy!"

"Oh, let's see!" Smurfette crowded around with the others.

"Well done!" Brainy praised his friend.

"Wait a minute," Gutsy told everyone, propping the book right side up so everyone could see it. "There we go."

"*L'Histoire des Schtroumpfs*," Brainy read. "Hmmm. Peyo," Brainy repeated the author's name, wondering if it rang any bells.

With a huge grin, Papa opened the book. The Smurfs were all surprised to discover drawings of themselves across the dusty pages.

"That's us." Smurfette pointed at the page.

Papa blew off a layer of gray dust. "Yes, this is the one." He began to flip through the chapters.

"That's so neat!" Smurfette exclaimed, excited by seeing the Smurfs in print.

Grouchy asked Papa to stop at a drawing of himself. "Am I really that fat?" he inquired.

"The secret runes are hidden in the drawings!" Papa told them, searching for them through the pages.

"You see all that in there?" Grouchy asked, confused. All he could see were drawings of themselves!

"Look here, at the patterns on this page." Papa gave them all a quick lesson in runes.

"Whoa!" Brainy said, seeing the page in a whole different way.

"Look at that!" Gutsy agreed.

"Wow," Smurfette blurted out, too shocked to say much more.

Grouchy just shook his head. "Well, I'll be smurfed!"

Gargamel stood outside the bookstore glaring at the door's lock. "Openous–lockicuss," he incanted, and the lock opened with a soft click.

Gargamel, impressed with himself, winked at Azrael. The cat winked back.

"Meow," Azrael alerted his master as they entered the store.

"What?"

Azrael showed Gargamel a large dragon-headed wand. "Oooh," the wizard gushed. "You're right, Azrael. This just has 'me' written all over it."

Gargamel took the wand. He opened his signet ring and poured the last drop of Smurf essence into the dragon's mouth.

The dragon's eyes glowed and the wand cracked with electric blue energy.

"Oh, that's just plain naughty," Gargamel exclaimed, and then began his search for the Smurfs.

In a different part of the store, Papa had just located the spell he needed. He quickly copied it on a piece of paper. "I think that's it. Done," Papa said. "All that remains now is to return to the waterfall and invoke this spell—tonight."

"And that will smurf us a Blue Moon?" Brainy asked.

Papa nodded. "And open the portal."

"And we can go home?" Smurfette asked.

That one was easy to answer. "And we can go home," he told his little ones, positively.

Just then the large sinister shadows of the wizard and his cat fell over the happy Smurfs. "Oh, you're going home, all right," Gargamel chirped. "To a little place I like to call Bellveedaray Castle—where your essence shall finally be mine!"

Chapter 19

"The dragon wand!" Papa cried out with dread. He had seen that wand—and the horrors it could cause—in the vision he had back at Smurf Village.

"No!" Smurfette shrieked, in shock.

"It's G-G-G—" Brainy was unable to spit out the wizard's name.

"Please, allow me." Gargamel put on his Smurf-imitation voice. "Ahh! It's Gargamel!!"

"Run, Smurfs!" Papa Smurf shouted.

"Come on, Smurfs!" Gutsy said, taking charge.

They scrambled to get free. "To the door!" they shouted.

"Smurfentine! Smurfentine!" Papa commanded.

The Smurfs scattered like snakes, swirling around corners and bends to get away from the evil sorcerer.

"Hurry!" Smurfette charged.

Gargamel laughed as he watched them flee. "Yes, yes. Do resist, little Smurfs. What's the hunt without the thrill?" With a staccato chuckle, Gargamel raised his new wand and . . .

ZAM! A bolt of blue energy rocketed toward the Smurfs.

Papa grabbed a feng shui mirror and managed to deflect the energy, forcing it to instead strike a large bookcase. Books hailed down around Gargamel, slowing him just long enough for the Smurfs to reach a metal grate in the floor.

"Come on, Smurfs!" Gutsy knew the grate was their way out.

"Faster, faster!" Brainy called to them.

Gutsy removed the vent covering to reveal a pipe. "Let's get out of here!"

"Brainy, take the spell," Papa called out, rushing over to hand him the paper as the other Smurfs made their way down into the vent. "Brew the potion and Smurf the moon tonight. It has to be tonight!"

"Me?" Brainy stared down at the page. "Smurf the moon? No, no, I'm not ready!"

"You're ready. I know you are," Papa replied confidently.

Brainy didn't look so certain.

As Gargamel's clomping footsteps came closer and closer, Papa shoved Brainy down the drain after the others. "Go!"

"Papa!" Smurfette called out from underground.

"Go!" Papa told her.

"Papa . . ." Grouchy was reluctant as well.

"Just go!" Papa yelled, emphatically. "And no matter what happens, don't you come back for me."

"What?" Gutsy called out.

Until that moment they hadn't realized that Papa wasn't joining them. But it soon became painfully clear that Papa was willing to sacrifice himself to Gargamel so that his little Smurfs could escape safely.

"Papa, no!" Smurfette pleaded.

"Papa!" Grouchy called out, helpless.

Once the Smurfs were all safely in the vent pipe, Papa marched straight up to Gargamel, showing no fear. "What are you waiting for, Gargamel?" Papa asked.

"Come to Papa." Gargamel raised the dragon wand. "Papa!"

ZZAAM!

The blue energy hit Papa Smurf. He froze, like a statue. The Smurfs, who were peering through the holes in the grate, screamed in unison.

Though he was frozen in midair, Papa was still able to speak. "Just go!" he commanded the Smurfs.

"Papa! Nooo!" Smurfette cried out, still watching through the grate cover.

Finally, Gutsy took charge. "Do as Papa said," he commanded the others in a firm but gentle tone.

"Papa," Smurfette echoed one last time, her voice as scared and helpless as small child's. Gutsy literally had to drag her down the pipe.

"Is that all you've got?" Papa taunted Gargamel, turning his attention away from the Smurfs.

Gargamel laughed an evil, evil laugh.

A little while later, four weary Smurfs slid out of the drainpipe and onto a moonlit street.

"What's going to happen to Papa?" Brainy asked.

Grouchy, who was overwhelmed with emotions, wasn't able to stay levelheaded. "Papa told us to Smurf the moon and that's exactly what we're gonna do!" he growled.

"Come on," Gutsy implored them all, "we don't have much time."

"Come on? Come on where?" Brainy exclaimed.

"How are we going to get back to Clumsy?" Smurfette asked. They needed to get him before they did anything else.

Just then Gutsy spotted a group of pigeons. "We'll ride. Come on!" In a lightning move, Gutsy grabbed hold of a bird and threw himself onto its back.

"Be still, bird!" he told the pigeon before calling to the others to jump on birds too.

"I don't think they're friendly," Grouchy insisted, examining the birds.

"Well neither am I," Gutsy replied.

"Do they carry disease?" Brainy asked, nervous.

But no one else seemed the least bit concerned. Smurfette, Grouchy, and Gutsy climbed on birds of their own.

"Hiya!" Gutsy commanded. "On, Smurfs! Let's ride!"

"Come on!" Smurfette told her bird, holding on tightly to its feathers.

But Brainy refused to get on. "I'm not sure I can do this!"

Suddenly a pigeon flew by and scooped up Brainy with her feet.

"You can do it, Brainy! Hold on!" Smurfette told him as the birds all took flight.

Brainy's voice echoed across the sky. "According to my calculations, this is dangerous!"

Back at the Winslows' apartment, Grace and Clumsy were sitting in the kitchen talking. "It's getting dark," Clumsy said, peering out the window. He was concerned about his friends.

"Yeah, we better go look for them," Grace suggested.

"Yeah," Clumsy agreed.

As Grace headed to the apartment door, it opened. To her surprise, Patrick was on his way inside.

"Hi," he said, unsure of how to begin telling Grace all the things he had to say. But before he could speak, he realized something: The apartment was uncharacteristically quiet. Looking around, Patrick immediately understood why. "Where are the others?" he asked.

"We think they're still at the bookstore," Grace said.

"Listen, Grace, I'm—I—" Patrick's cell phone rang. He checked the Caller ID then answered it. "Hey, Odile."

She was screaming so loudly in Spanish, Grace and Clumsy could hear every word.

Patrick tried to keep his voice light. "Listen, before you fire me, I know the ads that ran aren't the ones I sent . . ." He paused. "But they're the ads I *should* have sent you, the ads I *almost* did send, but I didn't because I second-guessed myself. I gave you what I thought you *wanted* instead of what I thought was *right*. But this is right. It means something to me and—I don't know—I think it's going to mean something to others, too."

With a glance to his wife, Patrick continued. "It's not just a moon, Odile. It's a Blue Moon. *'Once in a Blue Moon.'* That means there are only a few moments in your life when something truly memorable, truly *magical* happens to you." He smiled and barreled on. "And if you hesitate, if you're afraid—you just might miss it. And that's what that image means. Don't let those Blue Moon moments pass you by."

After a long silence Odile said, "Get over here right now and I will tell you if you are fired."

The phone line went dead.

Grace gave Patrick a huge hug. "I so smurfin' love you."

Just as Patrick kissed his wife, a flock of pigeons came fluttering in toward the fire escape window.

Grouchy was shouting, "Left, left, right! Right, right, bird!"

"Brace for impact!" Brainy warned everyone.

Gutsy gave a snort. "The window's open, you ninny!"

"Out of control!" Brainy squealed.

"Whoa, bird!" Grouchy's was out of control too.

Finally, Gutsy's pigeon landed on the coffee table, followed by three others carrying Grouchy, Smurfette, and Brainy. They all skidded across the rug.

Gutsy gave his bird a friendly pat on the beak. "That'll do, pigeon."

"Thank you, bird," Smurfette said, climbing down.

As the birds flew away, Brainy showed the others

the page that Papa had given him. "Look! We got the incantation!"

"Where's Papa?" Patrick asked, immediately realizing he was missing.

The Smurfs all paused. Finally it was Grouchy who choked out the horrible truth. "Gargamel's got him."

"What?!" Patrick asked, in shock.

"Oh, no!" Clumsy panicked.

"He took him to some place called Bellveedaray Castle," Smurfette informed them.

"He's gonna—," Grouchy began.

Gutsy stopped him. "Dooon't say it!"

Grace didn't understand. She repeated the castle name. "Bellveedaray? What is Bellveedaray?"

"Bellveeda—" Patrick figured it out. "He's taking Papa to Belvedere Castle in Central Park."

"To extract his essence!" Brainy said.

Grace put a hand over her mouth, horrified. "What?! We have to get him!"

"No! Gargamel's more powerful than ever!" Smurfette warned, afraid of what might happen.

Gutsy just shook his head. "Papa said no matter what happens, we're not to go back for him. He's trying to protect us."

"No!" Clumsy argued. "We can't leave Papa behind!"

"It was a Smurf promise," Gutsy told them.

"No, no, no. We can't," Clumsy repeated. He was shaking, he was so upset.

"We promised him we'd do exactly what he said," Brainy reiterated.

"That's right," Grouchy confirmed.

"I didn't," Patrick announced, heading for the door. "I never promised him anything."

In a flash Clumsy was on board too. "Neither did I. And there is no way I am leaving here without Papa."

"Patrick, wait. I'm coming with you," Grace told her husband.

One by one the other Smurfs rushed forward to join the rescue.

"I'm in," Grouchy announced.

"Aye. Me too. No Smurf left behind!" Gusty cried out, ready for the battle. "Not Papa . . . and not you."

The Smurfs raised their hands in the air, fists touching. "All for one and one for Smurf!"

Together they bounded out the door to save their Papa.

Chapter 20

Meanwhile a very cheerful Gargamel was singing a new song as he worked downstairs in the dungeon of Belvedere Castle.

"Oh, I'll squeeze a few and tweeze a few and steal their essence blue. . . . Ha!"

Candles flickered, casting dim light on the Smurfalator machine. From a spout, blue essence dripped into a vial.

Papa was tied to a chair, his beard partially shaved.

"Oh, very impressive, my dear, sweet, little Papa," Gargamel began. "Just a tiny little bit of your tiny little beard yields me all this essence!"

Very carefully Gargamel poured the essence down the mouth of his dragon wand. The eyes glowed even more brightly than before. "Just imagine what I'll be able to extract from your entire family of Smurfs."

"Alakazookas!" With a show of power, Gargamel aimed his wand at a stack of old and grubby wicker chairs in the dungeon corner.

WAZAAM!

"Behold! My glorious Smurf Magic Machine!"

All of Gargamel's rusty equipment suddenly became shiny and new. The chairs transformed into mushroom-shaped Smurf cages.

The dungeon was now exactly like Papa Smurf had seen in his vision.

"No! The cages!" Papa exclaimed, recognizing them from his vision. He knew where this was headed . . . and it wasn't good.

"How do you like me now?" Gargamel asked, showing off his Smurf essence factory.

"You're a fool, Gargamel. My Smurfs are well on their way home by now."

Even though Papa hoped his words were true, his visioning spell had shown him that that hope was quite slim. Sure enough, outside the castle at that very moment, Patrick, Elway, and a small gang of Smurfs were steadily approaching Gargamel's secret hideaway, a full moon illuminating their path.

While Patrick prepared to execute his part of the plan outside the castle, Grace was in another part of the park, waiting for her cue. She was standing at a kiosk filling helium balloons. When the time was right, Grace let the balloons fly free, up and up. Tied to the strings was a bowling ball.

"Good luck, Gutsy," Grace whispered into the night air. "I'll see you there."

In another section of the park, Gutsy was getting ready for his part of the plan. He was going to pilot Patrick's remote-controlled helicopter—just like he had in Patrick's office. He had to hold on to the craft with both hands, so the remote control was stuffed in his mouth.

When Gutsy spotted the balloons headed his way, he went into action. "Let's light this candle!" He removed one hand, causing the drone's balance to shift. The helicopter began to spin out of control. But Gutsy was undaunted. "Hey! Whoa! Ahhh! Ha-ha-ha-ha!"

After regaining command Gutsy raced toward the balloons. He snagged them with a tail-hook, then dragged the bowling ball in the direction of Belvedere Castle to set their rescue mission into motion.

Patrick and his crew peeked over the wall of Belvedere Castle.

"We all remember the plan, right?" Smurfette asked.

"Let's get our smurf on," Grouchy said, assuring her they were ready.

"Brainy, what's happening?" Patrick whispered into a walkie-talkie.

Behind the waterfall, where the Smurfs had first arrived, Brainy was stirring a boiling potion in a small pot.

Smoke rose into the air and sparks shot out from the

mixture. "I've added the ingredients and it's more powerful than anticipated. I don't think I can do it!"

Through the walkie-talkie, Patrick encouraged him. "Brainy, you *can* do this. Just say the incantation."

Nervously Brainy recited the words on Papa's paper. *"Par le pouvoir des Schtroumpfs, lune, deviens bleu!"*

POOF!

An explosion of blue smoke erupted from the potion. Blue tendrils shot up, wildly reaching toward the sky. As they hit the moon, it turned blue!

"I did it!" Brainy called out into the night, amazed. "I did it, Papa! I did it."

The water in the fall began to swirl round and round, revealing a slowly opening portal.

Brainy glanced at the distance between the portal and Belvedere Castle, where he could see the glow of a strange, evil energy.

How long would the portal stay open?

Would there be enough time?

Across the city at the Jouvenel launch, Odile was working the crowd, shaking hands with various celebrities. She spotted a famous chef and went over to greet him.

Suddenly someone shouted, "It's the Anjelou moon!"

Odile pushed her way through the crowd for a view.

The moon.

It was Smurf blue.

The crowd couldn't believe it. They began to applaud for Odile as if she'd somehow magically made the moon blue herself.

Back at the castle Gargamel moved Papa into the larger, fancier essence extractor that he'd just magically conjured.

"Now, I don't want you to worry, Papa," Gargamel said as the machine engine roared to life. "Remember, that what doesn't kill *you*, only makes *me* stronger. Ha!"

A voice from outside made Gargamel turn.

"Yo, Gargamel!" Grouchy Smurf shouted. "Come out and play!"

Gargamel was pleased. "Oh, I think our tiny guests have finally arrived," he said, rubbing his hands together greedily.

"No," Papa pleaded. So far, everything in his vision had come true. Terrible danger lay around the corner.

"Oh, well," Gargamel remarked, taking one last look at his prisoner. "Enjoy the ride, Papa." Then the wizard shifted the contraption into overdrive. Gears began to spin. Steam hissed and rose. "And remember: Keep your hands and feet inside the cart at all times."

Then, with a swish of his cape, the wizard marched upstairs to greet his guests, leaving Azrael to guard the prisoner.

Papa struggled inside the machine. He was trapped with no chance of escape. All he could do was shout, "Smurfs! Run!"

Chapter 21

Gargamel pushed open two heavy metals doors dramatically and stepped out onto the castle terrace. He carried his wand in one hand and a mesh sack in the other. On his face he wore a most sinister expression.

"Oh, Smurrrffffs!" His cackle echoed far beyond the terrace walls.

"You have our Papa!" Grouchy declared, leaping into position. "Prepare to get smurfed!"

"Yeah . . . what he said!" Clumsy agreed.

"Adorable." Gargamel raised his wand. "Two little Smurfs came to save their beloved Papa." He raised his wand and directed it toward the two Smurfs standing on the wall that encircled the castle's terrace.

A burst of light caught Gargamel's attention, and he turned to see what it was. Behind the wizard, on a rooftop overlooking the terrace, a match had been struck.

"Hey, Gargamel!" Brainy called out, appearing on the wall's ledge. "Make that *three* little Smurfs."

To Gargamel's surprise, Brainy was holding the match. Then, smiling as brightly as the flame, Brainy lit a fuse.

An explosion of fireworks lit up the night sky.

"And I went and got a few friends," Brainy added, proudly. Having opened the portal on the other side of the park near the waterfall, Brainy went back to Smurf Village and brought a whole army of Smurfs back with him.

Suddenly, Gargamel's secret castle was crawling with Smurfs! Lots and lots of Smurfs. Everywhere Gargamel looked there were little blue creatures.

Brainy introduced a few of the gang. "This is Handy Smurf, Hefty Smurf, Jokey Smurf, Panicky Smurf." He paused. There were simply too many Smurfs to name! "You know what?" Brainy said, on second thought. "I'm going to dispense with introductions. Let's do this!"

The Smurfs had come prepared with weapons: rolling pins, pitchforks, a meat hammer, and pots and pans. They were ready for battle.

But Gargamel was not afraid. He was thrilled! "My, my, my," he singsonged giddily. "The whole village must be here. Whatever will I do with all this essence?" With a wicked gleam in his eye, Gargamel raised his wand.

"On me, boys!" Hefty led the charge.

"BRRINNGG! BRRINNGG!" Crazy sounded the alarm to begin the battle.

"Let's get this hoedown started!" Handy declared, holding up his tools.

The smurfy troops marched forward and began launching their homemade weapons at Gargamel.

Gargamel tried to raise his wand. It should have been

so easy to take them all down with a single blast, but the onslaught was blinding and he couldn't see where to aim.

Narrator took his rightful place, describing the action.

"There comes a time when every Smurf must stand up for what's good and cute and blue in the world. And on this brisk New York night, that time is now. . . ."

"Hey, seriously!" Grouchy uttered, annoyed by Narrator's distracting narrations. It was a battle, after all!

Narrator apologized. "Sorry. It's kind of what I do."

But the battle waged on. Gargamel finally managed to raise his wand and aim at a group of Smurfs. But in the instant before he cast the spell, a sharp fork struck him and lodged itself deep in his arm. He moaned in pain.

Then Jokey pulled out an egg. "Eat yolk, Gargamel!" Jokey teased, tossing the egg at Gargamel. The yoke splattered all over Gargamel's face, giving Jokey the laugh of a lifetime.

Behind the castle, Patrick and Smurfette were trying to find a way inside so they could rescue Papa, but the back doors were sealed shut. They needed to find another way in.

"They must have locked it from the inside somehow," Patrick said, glancing around for another entry.

Smurfette found a drainage pipe, similar to the one they'd escaped through at the bookstore. "Patrick! Over here! I can get in this way."

Patrick took one look at the small pipe. No way he'd fit. "Smurfette . . . ," he began in a tone that suggested he was worried about letting her go in alone.

"Trust me," Smurfette cut in, knowing exactly what Patrick was thinking. "It's the only way to save Papa."

Reluctantly, Patrick agreed. Then he turned his attention to the grate cover, which was extremely heavy and difficult to move.

"Patrick, you can do it!" Smurfette cheered him on.

Like a comic book superhero, Patrick bent the bars, prying them apart just wide enough for Smurfette to crawl through.

As she lowered herself down into the tube, Patrick urged Smurfette to move quickly. "Go! Go! Go! Hurry!" he told her. "They can't hold Gargamel for long."

Out on the terrace, the Smurfs were still at war! They continued to advance, launching their homemade weapons at Gargamel. Every time he attempted to raise his wand, the Smurfs pelted him with everything they had.

"That's it!" Gargamel said, his frustration growing.

But it wasn't it. Not nearly.

Handy flung an apple with sewing needles poking out like a porcupine. "You know, one bad apple can ruin your whole day," Handy taunted.

"Alaca—" Gargamel had nearly gotten his spell out, when the apple hit him in the backside. "Yeeeooow," he exclaimed, accidentally dropping his wand.

While Gargamel pulled pins out of his rear, Handy pried open a crate filled with lipstick tube samples from Patrick's office. "Push," he directed the crew of Smurfs helping him, and together they managed to tip the crate, sending a cascade of lipstick tubes Gargamel's way.

In a flash Gargamel was able to pick up his wand, though the light in the dragon's eyes had gone out. He banged the wand a few times to restart the powerful Smurf essence inside. Back in business, Gargamel waved the wand at the Smurfs. "Aha! Ha-ha-ha-ha—"

But his evil laugh was interrupted when the lipstick tubes that had recently hit the ground began to roll around under the wizard's feet, forcing him to slip all over the place. As if performing a wild dance, Gargamel tripped and stumbled around the terrace, trying to catch his balance.

Brainy used the time to load a miniature statue of the Empire State Building into a toy cannon. "Hey, Gargamel!" he called out. "Here's a little souvenir from your trip to the Big Apple!"

The pointy part of the Empire State Building's tower shot like an arrow and made a direct hit. Gargamel howled with pain and anger.

Meanwhile, Baker and Chef were hard at work preparing a culinary attack Gargamel would never forget.

"Smashing," said Vanity, who was standing nearby, staring at himself in his mirror.

Baker and Chef paid him no mind. "Out of the frying pan . . . ," Baker commanded, and the two Smurfs released the pan, which swung like a pendulum from a rope, aimed straight for Gargamel. But Vanity accidentally caught his foot in the rope as it swung by and couldn't release himself. Instead, he held on tight and swung right along with the pan.

"And into the fire," Chef finished the quote.

Vanity, who had just realized the crux of the plan, began to panic. "I'm too beautiful to die!" he shrieked, covering his eyes as—*WHAM!*—the pan smacked Gargamel in the face. The sound of cracking bones filled the air as Gargamel pressed his broken nose back into place, allowing Vanity to roll out of the way unharmed.

Slipping out of the pipe and into the castle, Smurfette hurried straight to the dungeon. There she found Papa, struggling to free himself from the extraction machine. "Oh, Papa!" She cried, rushing to his side.

"No, Smurfette." Papa was worried more for her than for himself.

"Oh!" she said, noticing the straps that held him to the extraction machine. "What did he do to you?!"

"You shouldn't have come back for me," Papa said.

"I'm getting you out of here right now!" Smurfette replied, tugging at his bonds.

Suddenly, from across the room, Azrael pounced!

"Aaaaah!" Smurfette cried out, trying to fight back.

"Smurfette!" Papa yelled. He was helpless. He could only watch the fight.

"Hang on, Papa! I'll be back!" Smurfette threw a handful of loose screws at Azrael and then ran from the room.

Above the castle, the bowling ball bomb was being piloted in by Gutsy in Patrick's toy aircraft.

"Full smurf ahead!" Gutsy announced, alerting all to his arrival. "Charge!" he called to the troops below.

"Grab the wand!" one Smurf yelled.

"Get him!" another called out from the melee.

Gargamel, still dazed from being hit by the frying pan, hadn't managed to stand up yet, giving the Smurfs enough time to get everything in place for the finale.

A few moments later a buzzing noise from above forced the wizard to sit up and look to the sky. Overhead Gutsy and the aircraft hovered, the big bowling ball bomb carefully positioned over Gargamel's already aching head.

"Bombs away!" Gutsy announced. "I'm going for a strike."

The bowling ball dropped. At the last possible second, Gargamel snatched up his magic dragon wand and aimed the glowing eyes at the bowling ball.

"Alaca—ZAAM!" he chanted.

Powerful blue energy from Papa's essence shot out of the wand, blowing the bowling ball to smithereens.

Gargamel took a few shots at Gutsy, who successfully dodged them, until—*BAM!* Direct hit.

"Awww, crikey!" Gutsy's voice faded as the toy helicopter spun out of control, barreling toward the castle gardens in a fiery blaze. One Smurf down.

Feeling as though the tide had shifted in his favor, Gargamel turned his magic wand on the others.

Chapter 22

Strapped in the Smurfalator, Papa was growing weaker by the second. Smurfette knew she had to act fast, but that mean cat was ruining the rescue.

"Smurfette!" Papa shouted, warning her that he was in terrible danger.

"I'm coming, Papa!" she called back, then turned her attention to Azrael. "Get back, cat!" she screamed, firmly kicking over a box of tacks to slow his charge. The sharp metal pushpins scattered across the floor, and Azrael was running too fast to slow down.

"Meeeooow!" Azrael screeched in pain as the spiky pins lodged themselves in his paws.

With the skill and height of a gymnast, Smurfette did a flying leap and kicked Azrael hard in the face.

But that didn't stop the cat. The pins hadn't stopped him either. He came after her, claws sharp, ready to strike her down. With a leap of his own, Azrael landed on the handle of a shovel that Smurfette was standing on, forcing it to catapult her into the air.

Smurfette caught sight of a metal bar above the empty

Smurf cages as she flew through the air, and grabbed it to steady herself. When the time was exactly right, Smurfette landed with a *POW!* right on Azrael's back.

"All right, playtime's over," Gargamel threatened the Smurfs on the terrace. "Behold the awesome power of *me*!"

Gargamel pointed his wand at the sky and, moving it in a circular motion, he began churning the clouds above like a potion in an upside-down cauldron. The winds responded to his spell, blowing even stronger and whipping the Smurfs in all directions.

They clung to anything they could grab on to, but the storm was too strong. Soon, they were all swept into the tornado—completely under Gargamel's control.

"Help!" the Smurfs shouted out of the whirlwind.

"Now, I'm just a narrator!" Narrator cried out from the thick of the storm. "I'm useless in these kinds of fights but if you—"

Narrator was swept away before he could finish.

Gargamel opened the burlap sack he'd brought along and laughed madly as he plucked his Smurf captives from the twister with a magical blue claw that emanated out of his dragon wand. One at a time, he stuffed them into his bag.

"I'm afraid of the dark!" Vanity screamed as he was plucked and carelessly deposited in the sack.

In the dungeon Papa was very close to being completely sucked into the Smurfalator. A large pair of scissors chomped open and shut near the top of his head. It wouldn't be long before Papa was entirely extracted into essence.

Smurfette was still wrestling with Azrael, stuck on his back like a bucking bronco in the rodeo. Azrael tried to knock her off, but Smurfette held tight. "You're mine, kitty!" she growled. "That's it! I'm done smurfing around."

The two of them whirled wildly around the dungeon until Azrael slipped in a puddle of oil and skidded into the cages with a loud *BAM!*

Smurfette jumped off just before a cage door slammed down, nicking Azrael's ear and trapping the cat inside. Injured and defeated, Azrael finally slumped down and began to nurse his poor ear. "Meeeooow."

"You smurfed with the wrong girl!" Smurfette informed him.

"Aaaah!" Papa shouted from the other side of the dungeon, as the Smurfalator's giant scissors descended closer and closer.

"Papa! Oh no!" Smurfette dashed across the room.

"No . . ." Papa closed his eyes when the machine was less than an inch from his head.

Suddenly the Smurfalator stopped.

"Hang on, Papa!" Smurfette rushed over and freed Papa from his restraints.

"My little Smurfette," Papa said, his eyes brimming with tears of pride. "You saved your old Papa."

"Papa, we could never leave you behind," Smurfette told him. "Now come on, we didn't pick this fight, but we're sure as smurf going to finish it. Let's go!"

Papa and Smurfette rushed to the terrace.

When Papa and Smurfette arrived outside, it was a horrific scene: The blowing wind, the screams of Smurfs as they were sucked into the tornado, and Gargamel's endless cackling as he deposited each one into his rapidly filling sack.

"What's happening, Papa?" Smurfette was terrified.

"Nooo!" In a fit of rage, Papa grabbed a lobster fork and charged at the wizard. He held the fork like a spear and aimed it at Gargamel's leg. "Noooo! Gargamel!"

The wizard showed no fear. "Not so fast, goody blue shoes!" He turned his wand to Papa and with a flick of the wrist, froze Papa.

"Papa!" Smurfette shrieked.

"Now it's time to break their little blue will," Gargamel said to himself, dragging Papa to the center of the terrace, where all the Smurfs could see him. "Are you watching closely, Smurfs? Your beloved Papa meets his little blue end! Upsy daisy!"

Gargamel tossed Papa up and prepared to take a shot at him.

"Oh no! Papa!" Clumsy cried from where he was hiding on a parapet above the terrace. He was the only Smurf left, aside from Smurfette and Papa.

ZAP!

Gargamel fired his wand at Papa, and another powerful blue flame blasted out like a deadly arrow.

At that instant, Patrick leaped through the air, snatching Papa out of harm's way. The two of them landed safely behind a low garden wall.

"No! No!" Gargamel screamed out furiously. He began blasting holes in the wall until Patrick and Papa had no more cover.

"You again!" he said to Patrick. "Good-bye!" Gargamel raised the wand, focused on delivering two deadly blows at the same time. "I'm really—"

VZZZZ!

The roar sounded like a zap from the wand, but it wasn't.

The electronic buzzing was coming from Gutsy! He was back in control of the toy helicopter and came to join the fight. "This ends here!" he called out.

But Gargamel didn't see Gutsy, and so continued trying to finish his thought. "Really—"

"This ends here!" Gutsy repeated, louder, flying the aircraft lower and closer.

Gargamel still didn't hear the Smurf's proclamation.

"Going to enjoy this!" Gargamel finished his statement, raising his wand for the final death blast.

VZZZ—

Gutsy brought his craft even lower and hovered near Gargamel's hand. "Freedom!" Gutsy cheered, snatching Gargamel's wand and zooming away.

"Come back here!" Gargamel screamed, irate.

Everyone cheered Gutsy's daring maneuver.

Still on the parapet, Clumsy leaped for joy. "Go, Gutsy! Yay!"

"Get back here right now with my wand!" Gargamel insisted, waving his empty hands at Gutsy.

Thrilled with his success, Gusty raised the wand in victory. And—*WHAP!* The aircraft's propeller knocked the wand out of his hand, falling through the air and heading directly for Gargamel.

"Oh, crikey!" Gutsy moaned.

Gargamel leaped upward to grab the wand, dropping the burlap sack as he reached out.

Smurfs quickly escaped from the bag, running and jumping over walls to safety.

The wand continued to fall. It was just like Papa had seen in his vision.

Suddenly, Clumsy came jetting out of his hiding place, and ran along the high castle wall to try to catch the wand.

Papa sighed. His vision was about to come true . . . just as he'd feared.

Clumsy sprinted as fast as he could, and then he took off into midair, jumping as high and far as smurfingly possible. He extended his little blue fingers as far as they could reach. . . .

"I got it!"

"Oh, dear," Papa remarked, closing his eyes. He couldn't bear to watch the rest of his vision come true.

"Clumsy." Smurfette couldn't watch either.

"So this is how it ends," Hefty said sadly.

Even Brainy was pessi–smurfistic. "Our goose is cooked," he remarked, shaking his head in despair.

Clumsy was so close to the wand he could almost taste it. "I've got it! I've got it!"

But Papa knew better. "I know how this ends," he said miserably.

"I got it. I—" The wand hit Clumsy's fingers. And bounced.

All the Smurfs hung their heads, resigned to a horrible fate.

But then, just like he'd done in the video game at the Winslows' apartment, Clumsy reached out again and this time he grabbed the wand, spinning it between his fingers like a drumstick.

"Got it!" Clumsy fell the last bit of distance to the terrace floor, rolled, and landed right up against Papa's feet.

"GIVE ME MY WAND!" Gargamel's fierce shout could be heard throughout New York City.

He charged toward Clumsy, intending to take the wand back for himself.

"Ahhh!" Scared, Clumsy pointed the wand at the wizard.

Clumsy was thrown back as a monstrous bolt of raw energy shot from the dragon's eyes. The blast hit Gargamel square in the chest, sending him sailing over the trees.

"Whoa!" they all exclaimed together as Gargamel zoomed far, far away, deeper and deeper into New York City.

The Smurfs were stunned at the turn of events.

Clumsy wasn't so clumsy after all.

Chapter 23

Gargamel slammed into a pile of stinky, wet trash bags.

He wobbled to his feet and stepped off the curb into the middle of the street.

"How dare you!" he shouted into the night as if the Smurfs could hear him. "How dare you defy the great and powerful—"

WHAM! A bus plowed into Gargamel. His face smashed against the windshield. "Plooooshuchhh . . . ," he mumbled.

On the side of the bus was the Blue Moon Anjelou ad. "Smuuurrrfffs!" he cried out as the bus carried him around the corner.

There he saw Azrael, sitting atop a low brick wall by the side of the road, looking down on his master.

"Meow?" Azrael asked, raising his notched ear to hear the wizard's reply.

Gargamel simply groaned in reply—no, he wasn't dead. But he had lost his Smurfs, and at that moment he couldn't decide which was worse.

"Clum-sy! Clum-sy!"

A smurfin' party was in full swing at Belvedere Castle. Happy Smurfs were cheering his name, carrying their champion on their shoulders in a victory parade.

Grace came rushing to the terrace. "You're a hero!" she said, looking at Clumsy, eyes full of respect.

"I'm a hero?" Clumsy asked her.

Patrick came up beside his wife. They both nodded.

"I'm a hero!" Clumsy cheered. He swept his hands up like a champion, smacking the two closest Smurfs directly in the face, accidentally of course.

"Ow!" they both moaned.

"So sorry, guys," Clumsy apologized. "Definitely killed the moment."

"Clumsy, you little mook, you!" Hefty said happily.

Brainy interrupted the celebration, calling for quiet. "Sssh, shh, it's Papa."

Papa made his way through the crowd. "I owe you an apology, Clumsy. I believed more in a vision than I did in you. I'm so proud of you."

"Thanks, Papa," Clumsy said, giving him a hug.

"Maybe we should change his name to Hero Smurf! What do you say, lad?"

It took Clumsy only a second to consider the idea. "Hmmm . . . I kind of like me the way I am. Besides, we can be more than one thing, right?"

Grace was thrilled he'd taken her message to heart. "Yeah," she said proudly.

"So yeah," Clumsy told the Smurfs. "I think I'll stick with Clumsy for now."

Smurfette swept Clumsy in for a hug. "And that's the way we love you."

Grouchy had to wipe a tear from his eye. "I promised myself I wouldn't cry."

"And now to get rid of this!" Taking the wand from Clumsy's hand, Papa broke it in half and tossed the pieces over the castle wall. The ruined parts splashed into a turtle pond and sunk to the bottom.

The open portal to Smurf Village swirled behind the Central Park waterfall.

"To the portal, everyone!" Brainy directed traffic. He noticed that the moon's bluish color was beginning to fade. "There's no time to spare."

The village Smurfs gathered by the edge. One by one, they leaped in.

Handy raised his hammer. "Smurf ya'll later!"

"Good-bye," one said with a wave.

"Farewell!" said another.

Chef bowed, waving his chef's hat. "Auf wiedersmurf!"

Brainy approached Grace and Patrick, who had come to see them off. "You know, I'm not one for long good-byes, but I did smurf together a few words I'd like to say . . . aaaah!!!"

With a swift kick from both Gutsy and Grouchy, Brainy was punted through the portal midsentence.

Patrick laughed as he shouted after Brainy. "Take care!"

On his way home, Grouchy left them with a few parting words of his own. "I hated this," he began, then grinned, "so much less than I expected."

"Good-bye, Grouchy," Patrick said smiling.

Even as he soared toward Smurf Village, Grace and Patrick could hear Grouchy complaining. "Don't get me wrong, though! I still hated it. Just less."

Gutsy waved his arms up at the skyline. "I'll not soon forget this place. "Tally-ho!" Gutsy wiggled his behind, before jumping into the portal.

"I shall be back, Broadway! Toodles!" Narrator called out from his place on line.

While the others jumped through the waterfall, Grace and Smurfette said a sweet good-bye.

"Hey, girlfriend," Grace said.

Smurfette gushed. "Wow. I've never had a girlfriend before."

Grace held up her hand. "Smurfette. High four."

"High four, Grace."

They slapped hands before Smurfette stepped away.

It was Clumsy's turn next.

"And you, the little hero," Grace said, greeting her friend. "Come here."

Grace scooped up Clumsy and cradled him.

"Hero? Ah, stop. Well . . . actually, would you mind saying it one more time? It's kind of got a nice ring to it."

"Clumsy. What am I going to do without you, huh?"

Grace held him tighter.

Clumsy rested his head against Grace's shoulder. "I am pretty unforgettable." He winked and added, "You're not so bad yourself."

With a final embrace, Grace set Clumsy down. He took one last look at her, waved, and then went to the edge of the portal to wait for Papa with Smurfette.

Papa had something important to say to Patrick.

"Well, Master Winslow—thank you. You saved me. You saved the whole family."

"Actually, I think it was the other way around," Patrick replied and tilted his head, motioning to Grace. Kneeling down to Papa's height, he whispered something else. "But I got to tell you, Papa. That La La song—"

"I know, I know," Papa admitted. "Sometimes that song makes me want to pull a few beard hairs out." There was a twinkle in Papa's eye. "Well, I should get going. I've got a Smurf Village to rebuild. Your village has given me some ideas."

Patrick bent low, extending his arms. "Come here."

The two men hugged tenderly.

"Good-bye, Papa," Patrick said. He'd miss the little Smurf.

"Good-bye, Patrick."

Then Papa, Smurfette, and Clumsy joined hands and jumped through the portal together.

At last, it was Narrator's turn to jump. But he still had one more thing to say before he did.

"And so the Smurfs left the strange city of New York.

And I think they left it a little sweeter, a little wiser, a little smurfier. And as that portal began to close for the last time—"

Suddenly, Grouchy came back through the portal.

"Hey, seriously. Stop!" Grouchy commanded. With a firm tug, Grouchy pulled Narrator into the swirling vortex.

"Bye, New York!" Narrator called out before disappearing altogether.

Patrick and Grace began walking home together. The quiet was broken when Patrick's cell phone rang. "It's Odile," Patrick said. He answered. "Hey, Odile."

Odile was alone on the Anjelou rooftop, staring up at the Blue Moon.

"Patrick," she said. "I just called to say thank you. Finally someone has given me what I want."

And with that Odile did something she hadn't done in a very, very long time—she smiled.

Patrick hung up, feeling extremely satisfied. He glanced at the moon and then at his wife. "I think I'm not fired."

"Wow." Grace was shocked, but happy. "So that's a new job. New baby. Some unique new friends." She added, "You know, if you really want a bigger place—"

"Bigger? Are you kidding? Then we'd be farther apart!" Patrick put an arm lovingly around his wife. "Oh, Grace, I smurf you," he said with a huge smile.

Grace and Patrick kissed, and then walked out of Central Park and headed home.

Epilogue

A year had passed, and Patrick and Grace had had their baby. It was a boy, and they named him Blue.

Back in Smurf Village, it was time for Papa to once again forecast the future with his visioning spell. He mixed all the ingredients in the cauldron, and stood over as it brewed. Smoke rose from the potion and in the mist, images began to appear.

Storks flying.

Smurfs happily sitting around a table.

"So far so good . . . ," Papa said to himself. "Lots of smiles. And Smurfberries. Clumsy sitting still again. That's always good. . . ."

Then there was a bolt of lightning. The apparition switched from scenes in the village to a brand-new vision.

This time it seemed to be Gargamel sitting in a cage.

"Oh baby," the wizard said. "This time I'm on top of the world!"

Papa quickly realized that Gargamel wasn't in a cage at all. He was on top of the Eiffel Tower replica at the Paris Hotel in Las Vegas.

Papa shook his head in frustration and moaned quietly, "Oh boy. Here we go again."